Claire Hollis, Ph.D.

The Light

ISBN 0-9673122-2-1

Library of Congress Catalog Card Number: 99-096600

Printed in the United States of America

Published by Warfare Publications
PMB#206
4577 Gunn Highway
Tampa, FL 33624 USA
(813) 265-2379
Fax: (813) 908-0228
E-mail: WarfareP@aol.com
Web site: www.warfareplus.com

Unless otherwise indicated, all scripture references are from the authorized *King James Version* of the Bible.

FOREWORD

Dr. Myles E. Munroe
Bahamas Faith Ministries International

In a world filled with complexities, confusion and multiplied alternatives, we must have direction, clarity and sound counsel if we are to navigate through the fearful passages of life. In THE LIGHT, Claire Hollis captures the mysterious nature of life and provides sound principles and advice in the hidden lines of parables that are relevant to all those who read these pages. Proceed—and discover THE LIGHT that makes life easy to live.

CENTERVILLE, USA

There is NO LIGHT in Centerville! JJ and Lynn arrive in town prepared to rest and enjoy visiting with their nephew. Instead, they find themselves right in the middle of a satanic battle.

PREFACE

This book is fiction. Sitting in my hotel room while attending a conference in North Carolina, I began writing, with absolutely no idea of what was going to happen next. But I kept writing—with no outline or plot line. I didn't even know the characters until they appeared on the page. As unusual as it may sound, I "read" this book as it unfolded, and it was so interesting that I kept trying to squeeze time out of my busy schedule to get back to it, writing a paragraph at a time.

I was as excited as you will be when you get to the surprising outcome at the end of the book. What amazed me most was the way seemingly insignificant occurrences and characters that appeared at the beginning of the story came together at the end. I had absolutely no idea that the young waitress who appears in the beginning of the book would later develop into one of the main characters.

I am overwhelmed that God would choose me to write this book. It could be that He knows I would never take credit for it because I am the least likely person on the face of the earth to write a book.

I heard about a sign on the wall of a doctor's office that read:

God does the healing
Physicians get the pay.

This conveys exactly how I feel about this book:

God did the work
I get the blessings!

The Light

With its lush greenery, snow-capped mountains, bustling main street, and white church steeples, Centerville was a model American town, reminiscent of a Norman Rockwell picture. Freshly painted houses with perfectly manicured landscaping lined the immaculate streets and it was easy to see that, without exception, the inhabitants took great pride in the town's appearance. Even the automobiles parked in driveways were washed and shined to perfection, some with the keys left in the ignition. Keys in the ignition? *That seemed a bit strange, even for a small town!*

The fragrance of blooming honeysuckles filled the air, and occasional whiffs of freshly baked bread escaped through an open kitchen window. Even though the effect was pleasing, one quickly got the feeling that things were a little *too perfect to be real.*

One would think that strangers passing through Centerville would be irresistibly drawn to the small town, because of its obvious charm. It was beautiful, with elegant stores and clean sidewalks, and even the gutters along the roads were clean. But something was not quite right—it felt almost staged, reminiscent of the set designs for *Our Town,* an old play the local drama club had presented.

Main Street, a long street with a church at both ends, ran through the center of town and there were small wrought iron benches in front of the stores. The benches were separated by trees growing in perfect rows, and colorful blooming flowers rested at the base of each tree. Many townspeople came to sit on these comfortable benches because they loved to watch the activity around the center of town.

The locals read *The Weekly Times* faithfully, although there was rarely anything printed in the newspaper that most people didn't already know. Like many small towns, the people with money and authority had plenty of "little people" who were at their mercy and would practically bow to them. Few strangers passed through and when they did come into town, everyone soon knew who they were and why they were there.

Centerville seemed to have no problems but closer observation would have revealed that the Mayor was in total control and had ways of keeping the townspeople in line, just like a puppeteer pulling the strings on his puppets.

Mayor Casey was a short man with a heavy stomach hanging over his belt. His dark hair and thick mustache offset piercing black eyes which were framed by thick, dark-rimmed glasses. One of his most striking accessories was a huge gold ring with strange writing on it, resembling ancient hieroglyphics. Some who noticed it thought it had an ominous appearance.

Mayor Casey had a couple of trusted cohorts and the three of them comprised what was referred to as The Big Three—acknowledged as local rulers. Byron Van Cleve, president of the local bank, and Pastor Bob, senior pastor of First Church on the north end of Main Street, completed this triad. Even though everyone knew they were "in control," no one cared much as long as things in town went smoothly and problems seemed to stay outside the city limits. The important thing was the unspoken slogan: *Everything is beautiful here in Centerville!* These three men, Mayor Casey, Byron and Pastor Bob, were almost inseparable and spent hours together on the golf course each week, playing almost daily. They usually ended their day of golf dining together at their special table at The Lamplighter, the nicest restaurant in town.

The residents of Centerville knew that The Big Three attended a special meeting each month with thirteen other men and women who flew in by private plane and landed on the small Centerville runway. Centerville was too small for an actual airport, so they had built one landing strip just outside of town for small planes. The regular arrival of these "important" people was widely known, but the topic of the meetings remained top secret. Everyone knew *when* the people came but they had no idea *why* they came.

The meeting always took place after sundown and lasted about six hours—then the outsiders boarded their plane and left town in the middle of the night.

The church at the south end of Main Street, Centerville Christian Center, was similar to the one on the other end of the street. A huge steeple held a traditional bell that was rung every Sunday morning by Uncle Pete. Sweet, elderly Uncle Pete, with his thick white hair, snowy white handlebar mustache, and rosy cheeks was a mainstay around town. No one knew for sure whose uncle he was, but the entire town referred to him as Uncle Pete. During the week, he spent a great deal of time cleaning the church and took great pride in keeping it as neat and tidy as the rest of the town.

Centerville Christian Center's leader, Pastor Terry, was a tall, affable young man, gracious and loving, and extremely well liked by everyone who knew him. His father had served as pastor of the church on "the south end" for many years and Terry had grown up knowing he would one day become his father's successor in the pulpit. Leaving town long enough to get his theological degrees, he had returned home polished and eloquent, confident that he would do a good job. However, he settled into his role in a very traditional manner and preached the same old sermons year after year. Some of his parishioners wondered why he had spent so much money and time getting all that education—he didn't seem to apply it.

Pastor Terry's father had a brother named "JJ" who called to say he would like to bring his wife for a visit to Centerville. Pastor Terry had not seen Uncle JJ for many years, since he was a teenager, and he had met his Aunt Lynn only once.

After receiving the call, he remembered family members telling stories about JJ and Lynn doing some very strange things, something like "exorcism," someone said. Other family members referred to it as deliverance, but they all agreed that JJ and Lynn had become religious fanatics and had completely gone off the deep end, so to speak. Pastor Terry was willing to discount all this "gossip" and had told JJ and Lynn that they were more than welcome to visit him and stay as long as they wanted. Frankly, he found himself snickering under his breath at times at the thought of demons, because the thought of their existence seemed absurd to him. Yet the same time, because of his natural curiosity, he was glad that JJ and Lynn were coming. He anticipated hearing stories about people who were influenced by demons. Maybe JJ and Lynn could clear up some of his questions.

The church owned a guest cottage that was rarely used, but Uncle Pete kept it clean, furnished with fresh linens, and ready at all times just in case someone showed up. This seemed like the perfect time for a visit.

Across town, The Big Three were having dinner at The Lamplighter but they didn't appear to be in their usual confident mood. In fact, as they sat at "their table" that evening, they had worried looks on their faces. Word of the visit of JJ and Lynn Murphy had spread quickly around town, causing quite a stir. The Big Three knew they were expected to arrive in town the following afternoon. Instead of laughing and joking, the men spoke in hushed tones, and their usual air of authority and arrogance was replaced by a sort of subdued confusion. When they left, they were so preoccupied that they forgot to leave their usual large tip for the waitress.

The townspeople sitting around on the wrought iron benches noticed distinct, visible changes in some of the residents. People who were usually gracious and serene appeared to be quite rude and irritable. A few merchants came out of their shops and sat with them for short breaks and they all agreed that something was amiss. The very air seemed charged with a sense of unrest, bordering on panic! What was going on? Why the feeling of impending disaster? They could not explain it, but they all agreed that they could feel the serenity of their peaceful town being threatened.

The Light

2

Just after sundown, the familiar once-a-month plane could be seen and heard coming in over the landing strip, which they had nicknamed "Center Strip." The Big Three were so nervous about the meeting tonight that they had eaten very little dinner. Now they sat in their stretch limousines, noticeably fidgeting, waiting for the occupants of the plane to disembark. Close observation revealed perspiration forming on their foreheads, and even their breathing seemed shallow and labored. They didn't know why they felt so edgy tonight; they'd been to these meetings many times before. The three limousines would transport the visitors to Mayor Casey's mansion, which had been passed down in his family for generations. Like many of the buildings in town, it was quite grand in appearance, without visible blemish.

The plane landed and the thirteen emerged—seven men and five women. They all looked wealthy (exquisite jewelry and fine clothing) but the similarities ended there. They were quite a mixture: young and old, black and white, big and little, good-looking and not-so-good-looking. What could this diverse group possibly have in common?

Even to the casual observer, the leader of the group was obvious. She was first off the plane and her carriage and demeanor screamed authority—she was surely president of *something*. Lana, as she was called, was reed thin, cool and stern, and her appearance dazzled. Suntanned, with piercing dark eyes, she wore her black hair pulled back from her forehead and brought into a chignon at the nape of her neck. Her tailor-made suit fit her slim frame perfectly, and tasteful, yet extravagant, diamond jewelry completed her striking appearance.

The twelve other passengers swiftly exited the plane and piled into the waiting limousines. Within seconds the cars were racing away toward their meeting place, leaving a trail of dust behind them at Center Strip.

As soon as the sixteen arrived at The Mansion, they were ushered into the same library they always used for their meetings. They all seemed unusually uptight as they settled tentatively into the plush, leather, high-back chairs neatly arranged around the large, rectangular conference table.

"Down to business!" Lana's voice cut through the tense atmosphere like a scalpel. No one called the meeting to order—it was understood that when Lana spoke, *the meeting was in session.*

"Ever since Pastor Terry's grandfather died fifteen years ago, we have had complete control of this town. Remember how thrilled we were that the 'old saint' had finally checked out? He was nothing but a thorn in our side and nothing but death could get him out of our hair."

Lana continued without fear of interruption. "No matter how hard we tried, we couldn't get rid of him, so we just had to wait for him to die of natural causes." Murmurs of agreement could be heard.

"He was the last one in town to have *that light* shining inside of him. All we could do was watch it grow bigger and brighter. Actually, it was kinda strange, because when he first started believing in Jesus, the light was just a little glow, but my sources said that as he read the Bible more and more, the light inside him grew. Then, when he learned to really pray, and got stronger in the Lord, as he put it, the light got out of control and just completely filled him. I couldn't help but find that rather interesting." More murmurs, almost like a hum, filled the room.

"Yeah, Lana, we know all that. What are you getting at?" One man had enough courage to break in.

"What I'm getting at is this: we are being threatened again. As long as the old codger was walking up and down the streets binding our powers in the Name of Jesus, our hands were tied. It was a full-time job just to keep *the light* out of everybody else in town. But when he died, we had free rein and we got our control back.

"This is *our victory town*, the only town in the United States that doesn't have someone with *that light* on the inside of them. This little town has served us well, giving us the camouflage we need for our operations. Centerville looks so great and the people are so perfect and, best of all, there is peace and harmony. No one would ever guess that we are not what we seem. We've been free to do whatever we want without fear of opposition.

"But NOW—NOW, after all these years, we're about to be invaded by two people who threaten our entire kingdom." Lana's voice rose to almost a screech. "They're both totally full of *the light* and have already done us more damage than we ever could have imagined. My sources have reported to me that they are so full of the light that even our heaviest forces can't get to them. *They are covered with the blood of Jesus!* They invoke Him to put His blood over them every day and there are angels all around them at all times. It's outrageous! I absolutely hate that stupid prayer they always pray." Her voice took on a mocking, demonic tone: "Give me as many angels as it takes to hold back the forces of Satan and his kingdom. In Jesus' Name.'" Lana almost snarled, *"We've got to stop them!"*

Suddenly she paused and glared pointedly at Mayor Casey. "Can the three of you handle this or not? I want those people stopped and I want them stopped before they even get into town! They're due here around four o'clock tomorrow afternoon, so you've got eighteen hours to get the job done. Do you understand how important this is? This town is the only place left on this planet where we can meet freely without hindrance."

Lana gestured with one bejeweled hand to include her twelve associates seated around the table. "We put the three of you in charge and up to now you have done an excellent job. You have been able to keep Centerville free of even the least bit of *the light.* And you've been well compensated, too, if I do say so myself. But now they're sending in their 'big guns' and I don't like it! We're here to help you set up your strategy, but it's up to you to implement it.

"Here's what's going on. Most of you probably already know the names JJ and Lynn Murphy. Right now they're asleep in a motel near Lancaster, but we can't touch them tonight because angels have been dispatched to protect them. They plan to stop off at the old gold mine in Belville tomorrow just to sightsee, then drive on up here to Centerville tomorrow afternoon. Our Leader has given us unlimited power, and all the forces we need for the battle are at our disposal. But it would be a grave mistake to underestimate these two! Apparently they are totally filled with *the light* and they really know how to exercise their authority over us. This is not going to be easy!"

Pastor Bob suddenly stood up and blurted, "Let's plan an accident. In fact, let's plan more than one, in case we have problems."

Poor Pastor Bob. His father had been pastor of First Church (on the north end of Main Street) for many years and had been in league with this evil group most of that time. When Pastor Bob was only ten years of age, he had accompanied his father to one of the ritual ceremonies conducted by the thirteen when they had come to town for one of their monthly meetings. At that tender age, Pastor Bob had been dedicated to their evil Leader and he had made a pact with the devil. It had been impossible for him to comprehend the far-reaching impact of his reckless act and he soon almost forgot about it.

Pastor Bob had grown into an extremely handsome young man, standing 6'7" with blond hair, blue eyes and a graceful, athletic physique. Even more overpowering than his imposing appearance, however, was his charisma. He was gifted with almost seductive powers of persuasion, which he used to great advantage, and coupled with his good looks, he easily seduced women of all ages. More tragically, he twisted the Word of God, and although the whole town knew it, *they didn't care,* because not one person in Centerville had *the light* on the inside.

The others at the table looked at Pastor Bob but didn't seem to be persuaded by him; frankly, they all seemed confused. After much discussion, they concluded that they must do whatever was necessary to keep JJ and Lynn from praying the next morning. It was their only hope! If those two took time to cover themselves with the blood of Jesus and ask for protection from the angels, all hope was lost. So the problem at hand was clear: keep JJ and Lynn distracted so they would not be able to pray. This was going to take clever planning and fast action, because *nothing* kept those two from their morning prayer time.

The Light

3

Chime! Chime! Chime!

The gentle, yet insistent sound of the alarm clock broke the sweet silence of sleep. Lynn called out softly, "JJ, wake up. We need to pray before we go to the restaurant for breakfast."

"Oh, Hon, let me sleep just fifteen more minutes. Go ahead and get your shower." JJ was more exhausted than usual this morning.

Lynn grabbed the jeans and short-sleeved denim shirt she planned to wear that day and headed for the shower. She glanced down at JJ's tousled salt-and-pepper hair and large frame and was almost overcome with affection and gratitude to the Lord for this wonderful husband the Lord had given her so many years ago. Once in a long while, JJ was able to actually "sleep in" and she was glad, even though it probably meant that he was almost overcome with fatigue, which she did *not* like.

Lynn felt refreshed as she dried her short, curly blonde hair. She looked trim and younger than her years, and it was obvious that she took pride in her appearance. Suddenly above the whir of the hair dryer, she heard the loud ringing of the telephone, then JJ's sleepy voice.

"Hello. Yes, this is JJ. What's up? What! You've got to be kidding! When? How long ago? A police report? Tell me all you know. I can't understand you! Try to stay cool and just tell me what happened. Okay. I'll call you back in a few minutes."

JJ yelled at the top of his lungs, "Lynn! Lynn! We've got problems! Our house was broken into last night and whoever did it took Dudley. Come out here so I can talk to you! They either took Dudley or he got out of the house and ran away."

Lynn sensed the urgency in his voice, so she turned off the hair dryer and rushed out. She had heard the word "Dudley" and was immediately alarmed to think that something had happened to their adorable black, curly-haired cocker spaniel.

"What? Has something happened to Dudley?"

JJ. continued, "Mike just called. He went over to feed Dudley and found the house ransacked. Dudley was nowhere in sight and he called the police. They're checking the house now."

Dudley was such a sweet, friendly dog and he would follow anyone who would offer him a dog treat. He had been in the family for years, and had been their son Tim's pet while he was growing up. Lynn's face showed her alarm and JJ tried to reassure her. They both loved that dog, but they were also concerned about the house.

"Lynn, let's stay calm. We both know God is big enough to take care of Dudley, so let's pray. 'Lord, you know where Dudley is and who he is with. Please keep him in your protective care and bring him back home safely. Lord, dispatch your angels around him, in Jesus' Name, amen!'"

They hurriedly packed up, checked out of the motel, and went to the restaurant for a quick bite of breakfast. They said a quick "grace" over their meal when it arrived, then just sat and picked at the food.

"JJ, maybe we need to turn around and go home."

"Well, I thought of that, of course. You know I love Dudley, too, but I feel that we have to go on to Centerville, Lynn. We've been planning this trip for weeks and I know without a shadow of a doubt that we're supposed to be there. I haven't been able to shake this nagging urgency in my spirit about visiting Terry. We haven't seen him since he was sixteen and I owe it to my brother to look in on him. I just know there's some spiritual significance to this trip." JJ's voice was tender, evidence of his sensitivity to Lynn's concern about Dudley and the house.

"Just as soon as we get to Centerville, we'll check back with Mike and see what the police have to say about the house. He didn't indicate that there was much damage to the window where the intruders entered, and they can't tell what's missing." JJ was beginning to feel a bit of anxiety about "back home" but he was committed to their trip.

Quickly finishing their breakfast, they left a Bible tract for the waitress along with a generous tip, and slowly made their way to the car. After buckling up, they were on their way! Lynn was silent for quite a while before saying, "I think we should forget about stopping at the old gold mine, don't you? What do you think? My heart really isn't in to sightseeing right now."

JJ was preoccupied with thoughts of Dudley and the house, and he agreed, "Yeah, I think you're right. Let's just head straight for Centerville. We can drive around and look at the town, get a little lunch somewhere, and kill time until four o'clock. I wouldn't want to arrive at Terry's before he's expecting us."

Although the scenery on their drive was splendid, JJ had forgotten how treacherous the mountain roads were in this part of the country. So many turns, and hairpin curves that seemed to appear out of nowhere! They were driving along carefully but peacefully when all of a sudden...POW!

What was that? Suddenly the car swerved completely out of control and JJ struggled to stay on the road. When the car finally stopped, the front was literally hanging over the side of a steep cliff. What a dangerous, precarious position to be in! There was nothing but air underneath the front of the car and JJ and Lynn stared at each other in near panic.

In a strained voice, JJ spoke, "Okay, Lynn, let's stay still and figure out what we're supposed to do here. Let's not move...easy, Lynn. God is going to get us out of here but we have to stay calm."

Lynn hardly breathed for fear of tipping the car. The thought of having to open the door and get out without much movement was more than she could handle. *How were they going to do that?* Hot tears began coursing down her cheeks as they just sat there, silent except for their labored breathing. How could this have happened? What was going on?

Suddenly they heard a man's voice shouting, "Hold on, folks! Don't worry! We have a chain, and if you'll just sit tight, we can get it around your bumper without moving the car." They hadn't heard the truck stop and they didn't even want to move enough to turn around, but in their peripheral vision, they could see the outlines of two men approaching.

JJ and Lynn both breathed sighs of relief and JJ told the men to go ahead and work—they weren't going anywhere! They felt slight movement as the two men did whatever they were doing, then the man yelled again, "Okay, you'll be out of there in no time. Our truck is heavy enough to hold the car, so climb over into the back seat and come out the right side."

Slowly they did as they were told and quickly the men opened the door, grabbed their hands, and helped them onto solid ground. Then they pulled the car to safety.

It was plain to see that one tire had blown out. The men went to work on the tire and replaced it with amazing speed, then removed their chain from the car's bumper and got into their truck. JJ and Lynn moved toward the truck to thank the men when suddenly they were...gone...they just sped away without another word, leaving JJ and Lynn standing in a cloud of dust, shaking their heads in amazement. "Thanks!" was still on JJ's lips but the men never heard him.

After a few moments of rather confused silence, JJ and Lynn looked at each other, then Lynn said, "JJ, there was something very special about those two."

Speaking softly, in a rather dazed voice, JJ replied, "I know, Lynn. I honestly believe they were angels sent by the Lord...and you know what? We haven't even prayed yet today. The Lord really had mercy on us!"

As they got into their car and drove off, they immediately began praying, as they usually did every morning. They praised and thanked God, then they bound the forces of Satan and his kingdom. After they finished their prayer time, Lynn turned on the radio.

"Look at this scenery, Lynn. I'd almost forgotten how..."

Without warning Lynn raised her hand, as if to warn JJ. "Shh! Shh! Did you hear that?" Lynn interrupted JJ because she had just heard a snippet of a news report. "Listen, JJ! The announcer said that they just received a report of a terrible explosion at the old gold mine. Sounds like several were seriously hurt and some are missing. Thank God we cancelled our trip there today; that could have been us!"

"Unbelievable! The Lord has certainly had His Hand on us today. Thank you, Father, for your mercy and protection!"

The Light

4

Centerville was coming up on the horizon and JJ and Lynn were happy to be there, eager to get out of the car and stretch their weary bodies. They had never visited this small town of approximately 10,000 and they were astonished at what they saw. It was remarkably beautiful! They actually gasped at the glorious sight. Plants and flowers everywhere, expertly designed and groomed. It reminded them of the botanical gardens they had seen on trips to Florida.

They had admired the sight for only a few seconds before JJ said to Lynn, "Honey, there's something terribly wrong here. Do you feel it? I know what we see in the natural is almost beyond belief in its beauty, but what I'm feeling in the spirit realm is horrible."

A frown clouded Lynn's face. "I feel it, too! Let's get out of here! *JJ, I do not want to stay in this town.* Don't even stop the car!"

Pulling up to a stop sign, JJ reassured her. "No, Lynn, I know we thought we were coming here for a visit with Terry, but I honestly feel like we're here on a mission. In fact, I know it! Actually, judging by the events of the morning, the battle has already begun. And you know me—I love a battle! Remember! We're on the team that always wins! Stick with me—let's check this town out."

Even though Lynn knew JJ was right, she was hesitant. She had complete trust in God and had always had confidence in JJ and his discernment, but she was never eager to do intense warfare. And she sensed that they were about to engage in a real battle! However, she and JJ were partners, so she sat up in her seat, put her hand on his arm, and whispered, "Okay, Hon, let's go! I'm with you...and we're both with God!"

They continued to drive slowly down Main Street and could see people straining to get a glimpse of "the visitors" they were expecting.

"I guess we'd better find a restaurant where we can have a late lunch and rest until it's time to go to Terry's," JJ said.

They spotted an attractive, inviting restaurant and pulled into the parking place. "This has to be the cleanest parking lot I've ever seen," JJ remarked. "It looks like someone has actually swept it." They got out of the car and headed for the front door of the restaurant.

The faint tinkling of a bell over the door welcomed them to The Lamplighter restaurant, and they found the ambience cheerful and inviting (and, of course, *immaculately clean*!). They did not notice the three men seated in the back corner of the room at "their" special round table—but The Big Three certainly noticed them! Mayor Casey, Byron Van Cleve and Pastor Bob had missed their golf game that day and the waitresses wondered why they were sitting round the table with somber faces, making numerous phone calls, and arguing among themselves. They kept watching their cellular phones, which were all lying on the table, as if they were expecting a call at any moment.

At the sound of the tiny bell, Pastor Bob glanced up and his face looked like he had seen a ghost!

"Hold on to your seats, fellows. They're here!" His voice sounded almost like a wheeze.

Mayor Casey and Byron followed his eyes and they also got stunned looks on their faces. They all sat in total silence for several seconds, then the Mayor's voice broke in, "The light is so bright it's blinding me! There's no mistake—it's them! We're in big trouble now. Let's get out of here!"

Byron's voice was strong but filled with awe and fear. "Look at those angels—look at the size of them!" What they saw amazed them all. Huge male figures with wings surrounded the people with "the light" and the men (angels) had their swords drawn.

The three men were almost overcome with nausea and they got up with trembling knees, making a run for the kitchen door. Mayor Casey was dialing his cellular phone even as he ran.

"Lana! Lana! Our plans all failed! They're here! *Right here!* In the restaurant! Meet us at The Mansion as soon as you can get there. We're going on up—there's nowhere else to go!"

JJ and Lynn were enjoying being in this quaint little restaurant and were not aware of all the drama going on around them. They noticed the lovely young waitresses in their look-alike uniforms, gray with white aprons, pockets holding order pads. One of the young girls came over to wait on them. She was a cute, petite teenager with large blue eyes, dimples, and a long brown ponytail. And her smile! Her smile was so stunning that she could have done toothpaste commercials.

"Hi! My name is Susie and I'll be your server today. What would you like to drink?"

After taking their drink order, she asked, "Are you here to visit Pastor Terry?"

JJ and Lynn gave her with a puzzled look. "Well, yes, we are; how did you know?"

With a smile, Susie replied, "I'm a member of Centerville Christian Center and Pastor Terry announced that you were coming to visit. We've all been looking forward to seeing you because we so rarely get visitors around here. This town is so far off the beaten track that about the only strangers we get are relatives coming to visit someone. And they never stay very long, 'cause there's nothing to do around here. Well, excuse me for talking so much. I'll be right back with your drinks."

After their food was served, Lynn began to relax after the startling events of the day, although she still felt a bit uneasy. "JJ, everything seems okay here; in fact, it's so pretty. But I still don't think things are what they seem. Behind all the beauty and bright smiles, I feel something...well, I hesitate to say it, but it feels almost demonic. Do you think I might be overreacting? Let's say the blessing over this food; maybe I'll feel better after we get a little nourishment in us."

Susie watched as they joined hands and prayed over their meals. In fact, she watched them from afar the entire time they were in the restaurant, which was quite a long time.

After eating, JJ and Lynn laid down a Bible tract and a generous tip, then left the restaurant. As they drove to Terry's house, they again remarked on the beauty of the town and the surrounding scenery. Glancing up at the snow-capped mountains in the distance, Lynn remarked, "This must be one of the prettiest places in the entire world."

"Well, I know one thing for sure: it's certainly the cleanest," JJ replied with a grin.

After finding the correct street, they parked in front of a large, two-story frame house with a huge front porch. Dozens of pots with flowers and plants were spread across the porch, adding tastefully designed color to the gray background of the wood siding on the house. At one end of the porch was a large swing, and two rocking chairs added to the inviting arrangement.

Ringing the doorbell, Lynn felt an urge to turn around and leave when a tall, handsome young man greeted them warmly.

"Welcome! I'm Josh and you must be Uncle JJ and Aunt Lynn." He ran his fingers through luxuriant auburn hair and his blue eyes sparkled. "Come on in! We've been expecting you. Dad! Mom! They're here!"

Terry and his wife, Bobbi, came into the entryway wearing big smiles, extending their hands in welcome. "We're so glad you're here," said Terry. "There's a guest cottage over behind the church and we want you to know that you're welcome to stay as long as you wish—and please...plan to relax and enjoy yourselves."

"You must be tired from your drive. Why don't you go out and sit in the porch swing?" Bobbi turned to go into the kitchen, saying over her shoulder, "I'll bring out some lemonade and we can get re-acquainted. Josh, you can help me, okay?"

Josh, so tall and angular and youthful, and his mother, almost a foot shorter, with thick red hair and freckles on her nose (she also looked *very* youthful), made a loving picture, and JJ and Lynn felt a great tenderness toward them. Terry's father had been killed in a tragic automobile accident and JJ could see that Terry bore a strong resemblance to him, with his olive complexion, black hair, and tall frame. They were certainly an exceptionally good-looking family.

Time passed quickly on the porch and conversation flowed freely; it was a pleasant time of catching up on family news. After their visit, Josh offered to drive them to the guest cottage. "Dad tells me you're writing a book; I'm pretty interested in writing myself and would love to hear more about it. Dad and Mom thought you might be able to get some writing done in the cottage where it's quiet."

The cottage was charming and inviting, and JJ and Lynn were both ready to settle in for the night. "Boy, I'm exhausted. We need a good night's rest after the hectic day we've had, don't we?" Even though it was relatively early, JJ was ready for sleep.

Lynn yawned sleepily and agreed, "I'm tired, too, Honey, but we forgot to call home to see if they've found Dudley."

"You're right—I'll call right now." JJ dialed the familiar number. "Mike? This is JJ. What?... Say that again!... Fantastic! Great news! Thanks, Mike. Yeah, I'll tell Lynn right away. Here's our number in case you need us again. Yeah, I know we need a cell phone; maybe I'll get one when we get home."

Lynn could hardly contain herself. "What? Tell me!"

"Well, Mike said that two men knocked on his door today and they had Dudley with them. They found him wandering around and the police told them who to contact. They want to take care of Dudley until we get back and even though Mike told them we'd be out of town for quite a while, they insisted."

Lynn heaved a big sigh of relief before replying, "JJ, let's think about this for a moment. God has really protected us today in so many ways. First, the horrible accident at the gold mine, then that unbelievable accident with the car and now this. I'm just so thankful Dudley is all right." Her voice broke and she felt tears starting to well up in her eyes. "We have so much to be thankful for; we need to thank Him right now."

They sat on the bed, held hands and began to praise and thank God for His many blessings. Then JJ led in prayer, "Father, I ask you in the Name of Jesus, to dispatch (and we dispatch them right now with our voices) mighty warring angels around our bed, our property at home, this property, and our car, to hold back the forces of Satan and his kingdom while we sleep.

"Satan, I bind you and your entire kingdom in the Name of Jesus, that you can have nothing to do with us, our properties, or our vehicle while we sleep. If there are evil spirits in or around this property, we bind you and cover you with the blood of Jesus and command you to go back where you came from, in Jesus' Name.

"I cover our minds, brains, and memories, conscious, unconscious, and subconscious, with the blood of Jesus. Lord, protect our families, wherever they are, and protect our dear pastor and his family. Give us supernatural good rest, speak to us through our dreams, and let us wake up refreshed.

"I cover our home, above—below—and all sides, with the blood of Jesus and speak peace upon all of us. In Jesus' Name, AMEN!"

The Light

5

As JJ and Lynn drifted off into peaceful sleep, they had no idea what was happening in Centerville right then. Up on the hill at The Mansion sat Mayor Casey, Byron, Pastor Bob, Lana and the other mysterious visitors, who had flown back into town that afternoon for this "emergency" meeting.

Lana stood up to her full height and her eyes were blazing, darting back and forth, forming little slits. She was absolutely livid and her features contorted into a hideous snarl. As she pursed her lips, one could almost imagine her red lips dripping with the blood of her enemies. She might be a mere size four, but her presence at this moment was as menacing as an angry, ten-foot, hungry bear. The room was silent except for her voice, which made a hissing sound as she spat out her words.

"Men and women, we lost our first battle today. I have to concede that—but make no mistake—WE WILL WIN THIS WAR! We're back here to set a new plan into action. We're all going to have to stay right here in Centerville until those two sleeping over at the cottage by the church are crushed. As soon as we get through with this meeting, I want you to call home and let your families know you'll be away for an extended stay. Tell your spouses to get your clothes packed and our pilot will pick them up tomorrow.

"Mayor Casey, we're going to need a cover in order to have our base of operations, so I've already thought up part of the plan. Get the word out in town that you and the city council approved a new housing development going up on the north side. Let everyone know that you have brought in a team of real estate developers, financial advisors, architects, and contractors. Byron, you can back him up by taking loan applications through your bank. Pastor Bob, spread the word through your congregation."

Byron, functioning in his usual efficient, thoughtful manner, asked, "How is all this going to be financed, Lana?"

Lana gave him a swift, scathing look. "Everything is well financed, Byron. Don't worry about it—just do as you're told. I'll supply the details." She could be so patronizing at times that it was infuriating, but one had no choice but to just be quiet and endure it. "We have unlimited resources available to us and we're going to need a lot of money because WE CANNOT FAIL." She looked around the room to be sure what she had just said was sinking in. "We have a mission and no matter what it takes, we *will* succeed.

"What is our mission? Just this: JJ and Lynn are not to leave Centerville alive! There's too much at stake here and those two have already done more damage to our kingdom than any other humans we know about.

"Our greatest strength in the past has been that most Christians don't have the slightest idea of Who lives inside them. One of our biggest advantages has been that they don't recognize the power of Christ. They walk around in some sort of "La La Land" with no comprehension whatsoever of our presence. We've been able to hold them back, lull them to sleep, and keep them ignorant of our tactics. Even when they accept Christ, we've been able to keep *the light* from growing inside them because we keep them from reading the Bible and praying, and prevent them from fellowship with Christians who have more light than they do."

Lana's voice had calmed down to a more conversational tone. "They don't know how to war against us because they don't know who we are or how we operate. How could they? Most of them don't even know we exist! And that's the way it has to stay. I've been told about the book JJ and Lynn are writing and if it gets published, we could be put out of business altogether! It's one thing to have two people binding up our power, but can you imagine what will happen if Christians all over the world begin to do it? This book would go a long way toward exposing us to the world, so it just *cannot be published.* If these Christian humans ever discover that the Christ (the Holy Spirit) that lives in them has all power and all authority over us, then we don't have a chance. They'll win the war!

"I'm sure you all know that we have to bow our knee to any Christian who discovers his authority in Christ. So we absolutely *cannot* let this book be published! Our mission is to get rid of JJ, Lynn, and that manuscript before that can happen. That book will bring the battle to our territory and we will lose. It's that simple. But we're not talking about losing—we're talking about winning! Our Leader will give us *anything* we need to accomplish our mission."

Pastor Bob spoke up, "Lana, what's the plan? I know we can't waste a lot of time, but we..."

Lana rudely interrupted him in that infuriating, condescending tone of voice, "I've already got the strategy figured out and we're going to use something simple that has always worked in the past. Humans are so silly that they fall for the same thing over and over. This time we're going to start with *lust*."

"Lust? With JJ and Lynn?" There was a ripple of exclamations at such a possibility.

"No, of course not with *those* two. But we can work very effectively in all the people around them. It's really simple: we're going to get Pastor Terry's entire family completely bound up by the demonic strongholds we have so strategically placed in them down through the years. They'll be so caught up in their own lives that they won't even listen to JJ and Lynn when they try to talk to them about Jesus."

Now that the strategic planning had started, everyone seemed more relaxed and involved. Lana had been so intense at the beginning of the meeting (and The Big Three had been so hyper after seeing *the light)* that they all had needed to settle back and try to get a grip on what was happening.

"How do we start?"

"We start with Pastor Terry. We're going to infiltrate his church and dump huge sums of money in the offering. Sorry, Pastor Bob, but you're going to be a major player, so be patient. The church is way behind on bills and Bobbi has been yearning to live in the old Tyndall mansion for years, but she's just about lost hope. Remember when we planted that desire in her heart when she was just a little girl? She would take her little friends over there when the house was empty and they would slip in the basement window and pretend it was Bobbi's house. We put thoughts in her mind that it was her house and she bonded with every nook and cranny that she could play in."

She looked at Byron, "It's going to be up to you to make things easy for them to steal God's money and use it to pay their personal bills. When they see how easy it is, they'll fall right into stealing and buy the old mansion. Nobody will ever know the difference."

Pastor Bob seemed to be waiting to hear his role. "Bob, you're going to get to use all your looks and charm (and your considerable experience) to sweep Bobbi off her feet. You're the expert at seduction." A faint smile flickered across Pastor Bob's face. What an enticing prospect.

Lana gestured toward a woman sitting to her left. "Darlene, we're going to need your daughter. Her name's Lisa, right? Send for her right away and we'll get her enrolled at Centerville High when school opens tomorrow morning. When she registers, be sure she gets into every class Josh Murphy is in, because Josh is her project. She wasn't given that incredible beauty and talent to be wasted. Impress on her how vital this assignment is. She has to become Josh's entire life—she's done it for us before and she can do it again."

The atmosphere almost crackled with excitement as the sixteen turned toward each other. One could sense the eagerness to get going—let the war begin! They were ready for battle and now that their objective and strategy had been clarified, they felt secure and confident.

Lana's voice rang out again, "We're going to hit this family from every angle. There is no way on earth that we can allow them to be empowered with *the light. LET'S GO!"*

The Light

6

Even though they had both been awake for quite some time, JJ and Lynn were still in bed. Lynn nudged her husband as she looked out the patio door. "JJ, just look at that view! With the snow on top, those highest mountains over there almost look like ice cream cones."

JJ stirred but he wasn't ready to get up, yet. "Hmmm... it's a little early to be getting poetic, Honey."

Lynn was impatient to get about the day, so she got out of bed and went over to the screened-in porch. She stood for a moment and observed two wonders of nature: squirrels chasing each other in the tall oak trees, and baby ducks following their mama down a winding walkway to a placid lake. The backyard was filled with colorful flowers (was there any place in Centerville that was not awash in flowers?) and Lana breathed in their aroma. "This place is like a movie set or something produced by Disney. Are you sure everything is real?" She grinned at herself as she imagined the animals suddenly standing up and breaking into song. Lynn often amused herself (and others) with her slightly sideways take on life. She couldn't imagine life without humor... one of her favorite gifts of God.

JJ finally bounded out of bed with a big stretch. He didn't exactly ignore Lynn while she was "expounding" as he called it, but she didn't have his full attention, either.

"I'm going to make some coffee right now!" Lynn announced to her husband. "Get the notebook, because we have work to do and I feel a lot of inspiration. What a place to work! We're not going to meet Terry and Bobbi until dinnertime, so we can pray and then get to work. I'm loving this!"

She had said the magic word—coffee—so now she had JJ's attention. While the coffee was perking, they had a time of prayer, then got out their writing supplies. Sitting on the porch amidst all God's creative beauty was relaxing but they were able to get a lot accomplished, as well. They had everything they needed right there in that little guest cottage, so they didn't have to leave the warmth and charm of their surroundings for anything.

After several hours, they heard a knock on the door. Before either of them could get to the door, they heard a voice, "Reverend Murphy, it's Susie from The Lamplighter."

JJ opened the door and invited her. "Come on in, Susie. What brings you here? Is everything all right? Let's see if we can scare up some lemonade or iced tea." JJ and Lynn were curious about her unexpected visit.

"I just couldn't wait to see you and tell you what happened," Susie excitedly replied. "I just left school and practically ran all the way over here on my way to work. I'm a senior and they let us out of school early for our jobs, then we get work credit. So I can't stay long, but I just had to see you."

Susie was talking very fast and JJ and Lynn were struggling to follow her train of thought. "Well, anyway, remember that little book you left on the table when you ate at the restaurant? Well, I stuck it in my pocket and put it on my nightstand last night when I changed clothes. I was just about to turn off the light and go to sleep when I noticed it and picked it up and read it. I have never heard anything like it in my whole life! Honest! I mean, it got hold of me somehow. I just knew it was true, so I read the prayer at the end and I really meant it. I know someone else wrote it, but I prayed like it was really my own personal prayer."

She reached over to touch Lynn's hand. "It all made sense. That story is so wonderful, about how He left all the glory of living in heaven to come here—and how He was totally sinless—and then He hung on the cross so I could be forgiven. That just blew me away! So then I prayed that prayer about Jesus Christ being the Son of God and dying for my sins, and rising from the dead and sitting at the right hand of God. Awesome! Cool!

I mean—I just had to tell someone. I'm so happy! I feel so totally loved!"

Susie's beautiful smile radiated joy, peace and love, mixed with a big dose of excitement! She was definitely very thrilled. "Do you have any more of those little books? I'll take as many as you have; in fact, I don't mind paying for them. I want to give one to my parents and my brother and all my friends in my class. And we have a youth group at church and I've just got to tell all of them. I feel like getting on top of a house with a megaphone and yelling this out to the whole town. And Josh! Wait till I tell Josh! Josh and I are a couple, you know." She looked at Lynn shyly, who responded with a nod. Yes, she knew.

Susie's joy was contagious and JJ responded quickly, "You've come to the right place, Susie. We have a good supply of tracts in the trunk of my car and I'll run right out and get you some."

Lynn felt a strong impression to talk to Susie about deliverance right away, even in the very baby stages of her Christian walk. "Susie, you can't imagine how thrilled we are that you have accepted Jesus as your personal Savior. You now have a new spirit living in you, the Holy Spirit, and He is like a light inside you. Right now, because you are so new in Christ, the light is like a tiny seed, and it is up to you to feed it and make it grow. Just like a flower seed, you need to water, fertilize, and cultivate that seed of light."

"How do I do that?" Susie's eyes got even bigger.

"It's simple but it's vital. You must read the Word of God faithfully, pray on a regular basis, and associate with other Christians. You see, we are made up of three parts: the spirit, the soul and the physical—or body. Your spiritual man is okay now because you are what we call 'born again' but your 'soul man' is going to have to learn to live in a new way. The 'soul man' is also broken down into parts: the mind, where you store your memories; your emotions, which control how you feel about people and things; and your will, which tells you what you want.

"When we accept Christ, Satan (who is our enemy) is angry because he has lost what he considers to be his territory, and he won't give you up without a fight. We don't want you to be frightened, but we are going to pray a prayer of what we call 'deliverance' over you so that you can be all that God wants you to be right from the first moment of your walk with Him. When we pray, any demonic spirit that is in you or around you, in any way, shape, or form, will have to leave. Things have happened in your short life that affect you emotionally, and those feelings and memories can prevent you from being all that God wants you to be. When we finish praying, you will feel different and you will never be the same, no matter how long you live."

"But, Lynn, I don't want to lose my memory—it sounds like I'll have amnesia." Susie's voice sounded very concerned.

"Oh, honey, you don't lose your memory in that sense. Your memories will all be there, but the sting of any bad memory will be gone. Satan loves to use people's memories against them, but he has no valid claim to you after you are delivered from him and his strongholds. Satan and his kingdom can no longer use any thoughts or memories to control you."

Susie lost her look of apprehension and slightly nodded in understanding. She was beginning to realize that what had happened in her heart the night before was just the beginning of something big.

Lynn continued, "When you said the prayer on the pamphlet last night and accepted Jesus into your heart, you received a new 'spirit man.' The devil knows definitely that he cannot possess you, but he will settle for a stronghold in your life. *Stronghold* is a military term meaning 'a portion of territory that will not submit to the ruling authority.' What's so important about strongholds? Well, they can keep your light from ever growing. Right now the light inside you is just like a little dim nightlight, but as you feed it, it begins to grow and glow brighter and brighter. I personally believe that the spirit world can actually see this light in us. Sadly, Susie, not many people's lights ever get very bright because of so many strongholds in them."

"What are some of the things that are called strongholds? What are they like? Do I really have some of them in me?"

"We all do to some degree, Susie. Strongholds are things like pride, fear, guilt, grief, jealousy, rejection, addictions, infirmities, lust, perversion—and those are just a few."

"Did you say you want to pray for me? I sure don't want any strongholds from the devil in me. It sounds a little scary, to be honest." Susie was so earnest and open that Lynn's heart was drawn to her.

"There's nothing at all to be afraid of, Susie, and just as soon as JJ gets back, we can all agree in prayer that anything that might be a stronghold in your life will leave. How can we be so sure? Because the Word of God says that the Spirit of God that lives inside of you has all power and all authority over Satan, and all those things must go. Let me just say right here that everything any of us do must be in perfect agreement with God's Word."

"Here comes Reverend Murphy now!" Susie was eager to start praying.

"Susie, you're going to mature in the Lord so quickly that you will probably be a five-star general in God's army before we know it. Once you get your 'soulish' man cleaned out, there's nothing to prevent your spirit man from growing by leaps and bounds."

JJ, Lynn and Susie formed a small circle and held hands. JJ and Lynn prayed a prayer of deliverance over Susie, and Lynn told her, "Susie, we aren't sure how long we're going to be in town, but I would love to have you come over every day before work so that we can study the Bible together."

Susie hurried off to work with a promise to see them the next day. She left with a bright smile on her pretty face and JJ and Lynn were delighted as they watched her skip away, like a happy child.

JJ and Lynn went back to work and before they knew it, it was almost time for dinner. Checking her watch, Lynn went out to the screened porch to announce, "JJ, it's almost time for Terry and Bobbi to pick us up. Better tear yourself away from your writing."

"Lynn, this is just flowing! I can't seem to stop the ideas!" JJ didn't even look up from his writing tablet.

"There's something special about this cottage, isn't there? It's so inspirational that my thoughts just stay fixed on God. I believe the Lord is letting us know that He wants this book out in a hurry."

Knock! Knock! Knock!

JJ finally was forced to look up from his work as Lynn said, "That's Terry and Bobbi now!"

"Hi, guys," JJ said brightly. "We're so excited! Wait till we tell you what happened today!"

He would have gone on but Lynn interrupted him. "Let's hurry and get to The Lamplighter so we can talk over dinner."

They drove to the restaurant in Pastor Terry's car and JJ made an effort to restrain himself from talking.

As they entered the front door of the restaurant, the familiar tinkling bell attached above the door announced their arrival. Susie turned around to see who had come in and when she saw that it was JJ and Lynn, she just beamed! Her whole countenance radiated joy and she was practically dancing as she walked. With a slight wave, she indicated she would see them in a moment.

The restaurant owner, Janet, showed them to their seats, and commented to Terry, "Pastor, this church member of yours has flipped out. Her joy is so contagious that she has everybody in the place feeling good."

Terry and Bobbi looked at each other with quizzical expressions and took their seats. JJ and Lynn remained standing as Susie rushed toward them and spontaneously wrapped them up in a big hug.

After everyone was seated, Pastor Terry spoke up, "What was that all about? Do you know each other? What's going on here?"

Susie quickly answered,"Oh, Pastor, I read this little pamphlet that they gave me and I asked Jesus to come into my heart!" As she spoke, she made eye contact with Janet and knew that she had to get back to her tables.

Pastor Terry still looked puzzled. "JJ, is this for real? What's going on here? My dad told me that Jesus was a great prophet, but nothing more. And he said that the things Paul wrote in prison all had to be written in code and sent out, so you really can't believe any of it. And all my seminary training pretty much confirmed it."

JJ watched Pastor Terry's face as he talked and felt a great sadness come over him. He knew his brother had not been a strong believer, but he didn't know how far away from truth he had gone. Pastor Terry continued, "Dad told me to stick to preaching about morality and kindness to others. That way I wouldn't stir up any controversy. And that suits me just fine." His voice took on a hard edge.

The familiar bell sounded again, making everyone aware that someone was entering the restaurant. Most of the diners turned toward the door out of curiosity. After all, in a town as small as Centerville, there were few unfamiliar faces. However, hardly anyone recognized the large group entering the restaurant at this time. Led by Lana, they strode through the door exuding confidence, almost arrogance, eyes darting around the room as if expecting a table to be ready for them. Abruptly they all stopped, covered their eyes with their hands, as if shielding them from the sun, and turned to exit. They had seen *the light* brightly shining in JJ and Lynn. Susie was standing very close to JJ and Lynn, so her light blended with theirs. As the group stumbled over each other to get outside, they appeared to be very frightened, and their air of confidence completely vanished.

The patrons in the restaurant looked puzzled. What an odd display of human behavior that had been. What was wrong with those people?

"Come on! Let's get out of here! We'll eat at Mayor Casey's house!" Lana screamed so loudly that everyone in the restaurant could hear her. She was livid!

Susie returned to taking orders and the others resumed conversing and eating.

"What was that all about?" JJ asked.

"Who knows? Just a bunch of strangers. Maybe they didn't like the menu," Suzie replied with unconcerned amusement.

Pastor Terry thought he had an answer to their identities. "They must be the group coming in to build the new section of houses down by Crab Orchard Lake," he said.

Bobbi was quick to comment on that. "Terry, no matter how big or gorgeous those new homes turn out to be, none of them can ever compare with the old Tyndall mansion."

Before anyone could reply, Bobbi seemed to be almost trancelike as she went on and on about the mansion. "The columns look like they're supporting the weight of the whole house and the driveway—oh, there's nothing quite like that long winding driveway. Terry, you know I love the way the trees form a canopy overhead all the way down the drive, and then there's the fountain and the hedges and..."

Bobbi actually paused to take a breath before continuing, "No, you couldn't possibly reproduce that house today. Just the entry alone is a masterpiece—the spiral staircase, the crystal chandelier, and those marble floors! Marvelous! Old Tyndall owned about a quarter of the land in this state, you know," she said, turning to JJ and Lynn. "No wonder he could live in that luxury. It's been empty for decades, but his heirs maintain it. We absolutely *must* drive you up there after we eat. What about it?"

What could they say? JJ and Lynn felt obligated to acquiesce, although they would have preferred to get back to their cottage and read a bit.

Just as JJ and the group started to rise from the table, Susie came over, wearing a bright smile and holding a pamphlet.

"Pastor Terry, promise me that you'll read this before you go to bed tonight." Susie's voice was pleading.

Pastor Terry grinned and graciously accepted the pamphlet, but he was rather taken aback by Susie's unusual boldness. She had always had a warm personality, and they knew her very well because of her association with Josh, but she seemed different in some way.

"Okay, Susie, I promise, if it means that much to you. See you at church tomorrow."

As the two couples drove through town on their way out to Tyndall mansion, JJ asked Pastor Terry, "How can any town be so spotless? I've never seen anything like this in my life. Centerville looks like something out of a book of fairy tales."

Pastor Terry quickly replied, "Mayor Casey has always been diligent about keeping the town in tip-top shape, and his father was the same before him. I suppose their attitudes and principles have spilled over into the entire population. It must be a *pride* thing!" His voice *sounded* proud, in fact.

Lynn whispered to JJ, "Well, now we know that the ruling spirit over this town is *pride.* We're up against a big one! That's the same spirit that got Lucifer kicked out of heaven!"

"Shhhhhh." JJ put his index finger to his lips to motion for Lynn to keep her voice down. He didn't want Terry or Bobbi to hear her.

They enjoyed the drive; the moon was full and cast a beautiful soft glow over the scenery.

Terry broke the silence, "Bobbi loves to come up to the old mansion. We come up at least once a week, get ice cream, and sit out on the old cobblestone drive licking the cones."

"It certainly is lovely," Lynn replied, as they came close to the mansion. "You're right, Bobbi, it's breathtaking."

Driving right up to the gate, the four of them spotted the sign at the same time:

FOR SALE
Contact Byron Van Cleve,
Centerville Bank

Bobbi gasped, sank down in her car seat, clinched her fist and gritted her teeth. "No! No! I can't stand the thought of anyone living in *my house!"*

Pastor Terry was visibly exasperated. "Come on, Bobbi, wake up and smell the roses. This is *not* your house and it will *never* be your house." He didn't stop the car; they hadn't planned to get out and walk around, anyway. But he definitely wasn't going to stop, now. He just wanted to get Bobbi away from there.

Obviously upset, Bobbi sank deeper into the seat and was silent the entire drive back home. However, JJ, Lynn and Terry did not allow her bad mood to put a damper on their conversation. They talked, joked and laughed in an effort to cover her bad behavior.

Pastor Terry left JJ and Lynn at the cottage, then tried to console and reason with Bobbi. "Honey, you know our home is beautiful and comfortable. Don't be so upset! We'd just get lost in that big old place if we lived there."

Bobbi was not to be consoled, however, and went directly to their bedroom, and quietly crawled into bed.

Pastor Terry was tired and needed to rest for the next day, but he remembered that he had promised to read the pamphlet Susie gave him. Frankly, he was intrigued by the obvious change in her, and he also knew that she would ask him if he had read it.

Settling comfortably into his favorite recliner in his study, he read with interest and noticed an unfamiliar sensation coming over his body. He felt his heart race as he became rather warm all over.

"Could this really be true?" he thought. "I wonder if I should just go ahead and repeat this prayer. What have I got to lose? If it works, it works! If it doesn't, no one will know I prayed it, anyway." Pastor Terry's mind became a battleground for a few minutes.

"Somehow I sense that everything in this booklet is true. I really do need to be born again, just like the Bible says. In spite of all my training, I missed the most important thing—Jesus died for my sins so that I can be forgiven."

Pastor Terry felt tears streaming down his face and he fell to his knees beside the chair. His prayer was simple but wholly sincere: *Lord Jesus, if You're real, I ask You to come into my life and take control. I'm sorry for my sins, my doubts, and my unbelief. I do believe that You came and gave Your life in order that I may be forgiven and spend eternity with You in heaven. Thank You! In Jesus' Name, amen."*

Terry was flooded with relief and joy as he finished his prayer, and he slept the entire night undisturbed, awaking the next morning peaceful and relaxed, ready to begin a new life.

The Light

Lana and her little band of conspirators (with the exception of Pastor Bob, of course, who had his own church to attend) made quite a conspicuous entrance at Centerville Christian Center that bright Sunday morning. The modest auditorium filled quite quickly with the addition of Lana and her twelve, Mayor Casey and Byron Van Cleve, and JJ and Lynn.

Lana and her crowd tried to appear interested in what was going on and they behaved themselves admirably, considering the fact that they were in a church service.

Pastor Terry stayed behind closed doors, as usual, until it was time for him to step to the platform and take charge of the service. Tall and handsome, he squared his shoulders, looked out at the congregation and began to speak.

The moment Pastor Terry stepped forward, a rustling began in the section where Lana and the others were sitting. They began speaking in undertones, noticeably disturbed.

Mayor Casey spoke first, "Lana! Can you see it?"

"Of course, stupid! Do you think I'm blind? He's got *the light*, all right, no mistaking it. Just what we need! Now we'll have to get rid of him, too." Lana was angry (again!) and could hardly believe what she was seeing.

"Don't you think this is getting kinda out of hand?" Mayor Casey asked intently. "There hasn't been any violence in Centerville for over a hundred years."

"Shut up and listen!" Lana hissed. "There won't be any violence. This one will be easy; we'll use his wife and her lust and we can leave everything to Pastor Bob and Byron."

Lana lowered her voice even more and calmed down a little. "Just sit back and watch us work. We're going to mess up Pastor Terry's happy little home some more through Josh, his son. We can't allow that light to get any bigger. We'll run him out of town with a huge scandal."

Pastor Terry was continuing to conduct the service in spite of the minor commotion Lana and Mayor Casey were creating. They stopped talking long enough to hear him say something about the morning offering. This prompted Lana to turn around and give some instructions to her cohorts.

"Okay, put in your checks just like we discussed, and mark them for the missions fund. Let's get this over with and get out of here. I hate being in the same room with all these bright *lights.*"

They were unaware that there was *another* bright light glowing in the nursery, where Susie helped take care of babies!

Pastor Terry was excited about the visitors and the sudden jump in attendance. Although he wasn't able to shake hands with them after church because they scurried out so quickly, he was glad they had chosen to attend his church that morning.

Pastor Terry was able to overhear the conversations of many of his parishioners as they milled around after service. They were talking about the new houses being built and how they were going to be making applications for home loans at the bank the next day.

Bobbi had the responsibility of counting the Sunday offering and depositing it in the bank early Monday morning. This Sunday she was in a hurry to get it all counted because JJ and Lynn were invited to their house for dinner and she wanted to get home and put the finishing touches on the meal.

Usually counting the offering was a reasonably routine task, and Bobbi slipped into the office to run the tape on the checks that had come in.

"No, it couldn't be!" Bobbi thought as she looked at some of the checks. "Surely these people put too many zeroes on their checks by mistake. This is incredible!"

The average Sunday morning offering at Centerville Christian Center was $1,000, but the checks Bobbi was looking at brought the day's total to at least $200,000—an inconceivable amount of money in this town. Bobbi quietly put all the offering in the bank pouch and calmly walked out of the office. Calm? Well, she appeared calm, but she was quaking on the inside. What was going on? She could hardly wait to tell her husband.

But first there was dinner to be served—and it was delicious! An all-American dinner of pot roast that would melt in your mouth, potatoes and carrots roasted to perfection in the gravy of the beef, served with home grown tomatoes, green beans, and deviled eggs. A feast in JJ and Lynn's eyes! They didn't even dare think about dessert. But, after a little conversation and relaxation, they enjoyed angel food cake, sweet, fresh strawberries, ice cream, and coffee.

While the ladies visited and leisurely cleaned up the kitchen, Pastor Terry and JJ relaxed on the wooded deck, admiring the mountains. JJ never got tired of the view.

JJ had noticed a difference in Pastor Terry but hadn't had an opportunity to visit with him privately. As he tried to figure out how to ask him if anything had happened, Terry saved him the trouble.

"JJ, I've just got to tell you something—I can't hold it in any longer. The most extraordinary thing happened to me last night. Remember that little booklet Susie gave me at the restaurant? Well, I read it and then, when I came to the prayer at the back, I decided to just go for it! I read it and really meant it and I felt warm and happy and full of love, all at once. The love just surged through me. And I've had the same love and joy all day. I'm so happy I feel like nothing in the world could shake me and I feel like the presence of Jesus is surrounding me and protecting me."

Little did Pastor Terry know that his light grew brighter as he shared his experience.

JJ could hardly contain his excitement and joy. "Terry, you were truly born again! You can't imagine how thrilled I am to hear it! But now we have to pray that any demonic forces that might have attached themselves to your emotions will leave, too."

Pastor Terry looked bewildered. "I don't have the slightest idea what you're talking about, but I'm willing to do anything to be sure I keep growing in Jesus. Do you think we should pray right now?"

Because of JJ's years of experience in deliverance, he discerned several things as he prayed for Terry. A tremendous evil spirit of hindrance was holding Terry back from being all that God wanted him to be. As long as that spirit bound him, he would never reach his potential in spiritual things. Also, a spirit of pride had come down from Terry's father, so JJ broke any ungodly soul ties that had developed between Terry and his father. JJ also discerned a spirit of fear, especially fear of failure and fear of the future, and that stronghold was broken.

Terry was open to deliverance and responded to the work of the Holy Spirit in his life. After it was all over, he said, "You know, JJ, I'll bet my grandpa is smiling up in heaven right now. He really loved Jesus with all his heart and he prayed constantly. But my dad told me that Gramps was a real fanatic and I shouldn't pay any attention to him."

Bobbi and Lynn had gone out onto the front porch to relax in the swing, so they heard none of what was going on out back. JJ could hardly wait to tell Lynn all the wonderful news and Terry was trying to figure out how to approach the subject with Bobbi. It seemed to him that he had become a completely new person in the last fifteen hours and he longed to share all the good news with Bobbi. He wanted her to be as happy as he was about his experience, but he also wanted to be wise in how he presented it. His biggest fear was that he not come across as judgmental toward her. "Give me wisdom, Lord," he prayed silently.

After JJ and Lynn had returned to the cottage, Terry and Bobbi spent a quiet evening exchanging mostly small talk. Then Terry excused himself and went to bed, falling asleep immediately. Bobbi joined him not long afterwards, but she lay awake most of the night thinking about the old Tyndall mansion—and the vast amount of money that had come in that morning in the offering baskets. Her mind became a fertile ground for the eager voices of the enemy of her soul.

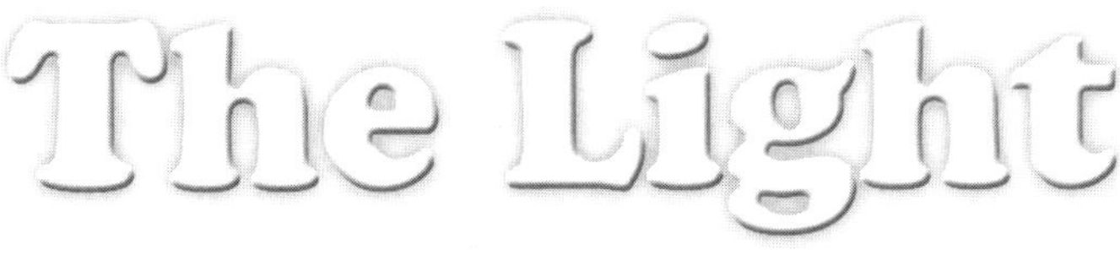

The Light

8

Terry and Bobbi awoke early, eager to get about the day. They always looked forward to Mondays because they got to relax after the pressures of Sunday's responsibilities. Bobbi was especially excited at the prospect of getting to the bank with that unusually large deposit.

Terry had received word Sunday that Uncle Pete was to go into the hospital on Monday for tests. "Bobbi, I'm going over to the hospital to visit Uncle Pete and make sure he's okay. Then I need to deliver some groceries to old Mrs. Walker. Why don't I meet you at The Lamplighter around noon for lunch. Will that work for you?"

Bobbi tried not to sound too elated as she replied, "That's fine, Terry. I'll make the deposit and see you later!"

If someone had been spying on Bobbi, they would have noticed her hurried exit from the house. She was so anxious to get to the bank that she arrived half an hour before it opened. She ducked into the nearby donut shop, picked up a cup of coffee, then went back to the wrought iron bench in front of the bank and sat down. She tried to be patient, but it was hard to wait. She wanted to get those checks deposited before Terry could see them.

Byron Van Cleve was already in the bank and saw Bobbi when he glanced out his office window. He hurriedly picked up the phone and called Pastor Bob.

"Okay, fellow, you're on! The spotlight is on you and you'd better be ready for action. Bobbi is right outside waiting for the bank to open, just as we hoped. Get down here and bring all your charm with you, because we're counting on you! Good luck—and hurry!"

Immediately after the conversation with Byron, Pastor Bob called Lana and gave her the report.

"Lana? Pastor Bob here. I'm on my way to the bank now, so I'll be *accidentally* bumping into Bobbi."

Lana instantly took control of the conversation. "Okay, I'll meet you in the bank parking lot in five minutes and I'll have a love potion with me that I just brewed. You'll have to convince Bobbi to drink it just in case your charisma doesn't work." Pastor Bob could hear Lana softly giggle.

After Pastor Bob and Lana had their little clandestine meeting in the parking lot, he walked around the corner to the bench where Bobbi was sitting. He had dressed carefully that morning, expecting the call from Byron, and was extremely handsome in his polo shirt and dress slacks.

"Well, Bobbi Murphy! What are you doing here at this time of morning? Looks like we're both a little early for the bank, doesn't it? Mind if I sit down?"

Bobbi indicated her assent with a graceful gesture of her hand and a subtle nod. Her husband was tall, dark and handsome, and she was very happy with him, but she had admired this tall, blond charmer from afar for several years. Imagine meeting him this morning!

Pastor Bob sat down, looked directly at Bobbi, and lowered his voice as he said, "You know, Bobbi, it's really great to see you. For some strange reason I've been thinking a lot about you lately. It's probably because I heard some women talking about you the other day, about how beautiful and young you look! I could tell they were a little jealous, although I'm sure they would never admit it. They're right, though. You really missed your calling—you should be in movies!" He wondered if his "magic" was having any effect on her.

Bobbi lowered her eyes and replied shyly, "Thanks, Pastor Bob. You're much too kind!"

As she bent down and reached for something at her feet, her face registered surprise. "I can't believe it! I must have left my purse in the car. How absentminded!

Would you mind watching my coffee for just a second while I run get it?"

Pastor Bob could hardly believe how smoothly things were going. *Would he mind*? This was the perfect opportunity to open the little vial and pour Lana's "potion" into the coffee. Poor Bobbi had no idea she was being set up and when she returned, she gulped down the remainder of her coffee.

"Pastor Bob, did you know that the old Tyndall mansion is on the market?"

"Really! No, I didn't. You know, I've never even been inside the place and I've always wanted to tour it. If the inside is anything like the outside, it should be a real showplace. Do you know the asking price?"

Bobbi started to stand and Pastor Bob took her hand to assist her as she answered, "I don't know but I see the bank's open, so maybe we can find out." Bobbi was a bit flustered and withdrew her hand from his as they entered the bank together.

Bobbie got in line behind another customer to make her deposit, Pastor Bob at her side. Becoming somewhat disconcerted, she was acutely aware of his presence and her thoughts raced as she noticed how appealing he was.

"Wow! He's really amazing looking! I wonder what cologne he's wearing. He didn't seem to want to let go of my hand when we came in the bank. I wonder what's going on here—if anything."

Pastor Bob knew he had to do something when it was his turn at the teller's window, so he pulled out his checkbook. After Bobbi made her deposit, he transacted some minor business and pretended to get ready to leave. Right at that moment, as they had planned, Byron appeared.

"Mr. Van Cleve, I was just going to see if you were busy. We took some friends up to the old Tyndall mansion the other day and saw the 'For Sale' sign. Could you tell me what they want for it?" Bobbi was so excited she could hardly get her words out.

"How are you, Bobbi? It's nice to see you. Yes, as a matter of fact, I do know about that sale. You're not going to believe this, but the heirs have been hanging onto it for years because one brother refused to sell. However, he died last week and a member of the family called to see if I would handle the sale. They are ready to just dump it."

Bobbi could hardly contain herself! "But what's the price?"

"That's the amazing part. They are willing to sell the mansion fully furnished for only $200,000 and we know that it would go for several million if it were located in a city. Somebody's going to really clean up when they buy the place."

Bobbi's desire for the mansion was almost irresistible and now that she knew the asking price, she knew that she could possibly see her dream fulfilled.

Pastor Bob spoke up. "I'd love to see the inside of the mansion, Byron. Is it possible that someone could show it to me this morning?"

Bobbi chimed in, "I'd love to see it, too."

To their disappointment, Byron frowned and slowly shook his head. "I'm so sorry. My schedule is completely filled today." Then his eyes brightened. "But I could give you the key and you two could go out there together and look around."

Pastor Bob followed Byron into his office to get the key without even consulting Bobbi. He obviously knew that she would jump at the chance to get inside the old Tyndall mansion—and he had additional plans.

Bobbi's heart was racing and she was flushed with excitement. She considered calling Terry to tell him where she was going, but she brushed the idea aside. She felt reckless and unconcerned about anything but herself and her wishes, and she didn't heed the tiny voice of caution that whispered inside.

Pastor Bob emerged from Byron's office holding the key to the prized old mansion, motioned for Bobbi to follow him, and headed for his car. Without really thinking, she slipped into the car beside him and off they went.

As Pastor Bob drove silently along the winding road, Bobbi became more and more conscious of his presence. She turned her head toward him and before she could say a word, she heard him say, "Hmmmm. Bobbi and Bob. That sounds like a good team, doesn't it?"

Bobbi caught her breath and just stared at him, concentrating on his beautiful blue eyes and striking bone structure. She wondered what was happening to her. She felt mesmerized and shook her head to collect her thoughts. She was so preoccupied with her own thoughts that she didn't even reply to his remark.

"Here we are, Bobbi. Look at it! I'm going to park right here by the fountain." Pastor Bob drove up as close to the entrance as he could and they got out of the car.

The majestic colonial pillars framed the entryway and they walked side by side up the few steps. Pastor Bob opened the huge door with Byron's key and ushered Bobbi inside. They gasped in unison at the splendor they saw. The interior was clean and obviously well maintained. It was vast and grand, boasting breathtakingly beautiful furniture, luxurious area carpets, dramatic window treatments, and marble floors. To the right as they entered was a winding staircase so wide that half a dozen people could have walked side by side. Bobbi felt like she had been transported to a land of magnificence and magic.

Where to start? That was the question. Even though Bobbi had been in the house as a child, it had been completely redecorated and was more beautiful than she remembered. Exquisite antique furniture looked comfortable and inviting.

Bobbi continued to stand immobile and Pastor Bob took her hand and led her into the parlor to begin their personal tour. Pastor Bob did most of the talking as they went from room to room, up the flight of stairs, back down and out onto the grounds. And he held her hand the whole time.

"Bobbi, you know the furniture and decorating alone must be worth the price they're asking for this place. Can you imagine living here?" Could she imagine it? That certainly was a rhetorical question—she had done little but imagine it for years.

Bobbi remained mostly silent, aware of Pastor Bob's hand guiding her, and feeling at ease with it after the first wave of awkwardness vanished.

Because of Bobbi's seeming unresponsiveness, Pastor Bob felt like he should keep on "selling" the house. "Look! Wouldn't this be a great place for guests? You could entertain your uncle and his wife here instead of sticking them in that little old cottage behind the church."

Entering another room, Pastor Bob continued, "And this would be a great place to have your monthly teas for the ladies from the church." Still, Bobbi was quiet.

"Bobbi, the swimming pool and the basketball and tennis courts would be wonderful for Josh. He could have his friends over and he'd be the most popular kid in town." Bobbi smiled for the first time. Yes, Josh. The house would be so wonderful for her beloved son.

Pastor Bob pressed on. "You know the women in town already envy you because you're so pretty and if you lived in this house, you'd have it all!" Pastor Bob was beginning to sound like the voice of the tempter himself.

"You can have the house, you know. All you have to do is figure out how to get the $200,000, or even some of that amount, and you could move in tomorrow. One of us has to buy this place! If you can't come up with the money, I'm going to buy it. But I'll give you first chance at it. What do you think?" He was skillfully enticing her.

While walking through the house, Bobbi had put herself in every room, dreaming of how it would be living there. She *had* to have this house. She *had to have it!* She just wasn't sure how she was going to get it—but she had an idea.

Bobbi was still silent and she noticed that Pastor Bob had not let go of her hand for a second the entire time they were walking around. Her mind was swirling and her emotions were a little unstable, as well.

Pastor Bob locked the key to the stately old mansion, took Bobbi's hand again, and led her toward the car. As he opened her door, he blocked her from getting in. She looked up at him and their eyes met, staying locked for quite a long time. Then he reached down, cupped her chin in his hand, tilted her head toward him, leaned down and kissed her. Bobbi didn't resist! Her response to his kiss surprised her, then confusion flooded in. Her rational self pulled away from his embrace and he released her.

"Bobbi, I'm sorry! I'm sorry! I don't know what came over me! You are so beautiful and...well, please forgive me! We'd better get back to town."

Back to town! Bobbi glanced down at her watch and realized that they had been at the mansion for almost four hours. She was late for her appointment with Terry and hadn't even bothered to call him on her cell phone. Also, she was confused and excited and flattered and embarrassed all at the same time.

Pastor Bob was uncharacteristically quiet on the way back to town and Bobbi didn't make a sound. She was stunned by what had just happened, and further dismayed and bewildered by the emotions she was experiencing. She told herself to keep a cool head because she had to do some negotiating on her dream house!

The parking lot was relatively empty when they returned to the bank and Bobbi was relieved. She didn't want anyone to see her driving around with Pastor Bob. He came around the car, opened the door for her, reached for her hand to help her out, and looked into her eyes.

"This has been the greatest day of my life, Bobbi! I am *really* looking forward to seeing you again." He smiled irresistibly and she wanted to reply, "Oh, yes. Me, too!" But she merely smiled and walked toward the bank. She had a plan!

"Is Mr. Van Cleve available, please? Tell him Bobbi Murphy would like to speak with him." Bobbi went directly to the area where Byron Van Cleve worked and boldly asked to see him.

"Mrs. Murphy, Mr. Van Cleve said he has a few minutes before his next appointment. Come this way, please."

Bobbi's face glowed as she sat down in Byron Van Cleve's tastefully appointed office.

"Mr. Van Cleve, thank you so much for letting Pastor Bob and me tour the Tyndall mansion. I've decided I want to buy it and I can pay cash for it."

Byron's face registered surprise, although this is what he knew would happen. Everything was going according to plan.

"Well, Mrs. Murphy, we'd be glad to do business with you. Actually, I had a contract drawn up while you were out there just in case you wanted to make an offer on it. I have power to accept your offer, so let's work out the details."

"How much do you need to secure the contract? Will $50,000 be enough?" Bobbi asked, as she made out the check. Byron accepted her check, had her sign the contract and told her they had a deal! Bobbi Murphy left the bank a very happy woman!

She looked at her watch again, rushed to The Lamplighter and burst through the door. The familiar bell sounded and Terry looked up and waved her to his table. Susie, the waitress, was standing by the table and the two were in animated conversation. Bobbi knew they were discussing something spiritual, but she didn't think anything in the world was as exciting and urgent as her news.

Bobbi knew she was late, she murmured the necessary apologies, and then blurted out, "Terry, I've got the most exciting news! Wait till you hear what happened!" Noticing that Susie had not left, she said, "Susie, will you give us about fifteen minutes, then come back and take our order? Thanks."

Terry looked a little impatient because he felt Bobbi had been a bit abrupt with Susie. "What's so important, Bobbi? I'm hungry."

"Terry, I just bought the old Tyndall mansion!"

"You *what*?" Terry stared at his wife in disbelief. He had never known his wife to do impulsive, impetuous things like this and he was incredulous. Surely he had heard her incorrectly.

"Bobbi, what on earth are you saying? Are you sick? We don't have that kind of money. Maybe we'd better go home and discuss this."

Bobbi laughed lightly, "No, no, Terry, you don't understand! We have plenty of money. I was going to surprise you at lunch today—and, by the way, I apologize again for being late—but things just came together so beautifully that I knew it would be okay with you."

"What are you talking about, Bobbi? What surprise?"

"Well, Honey, when I counted the offering yesterday, it came to a total of $201,000. Can you believe it? I wanted to get it in the bank and surprise you with the deposit slip at lunch today but something wonderful came up. When I went in the bank, I found out that the Tyndall mansion was for sale for only $200,000. And that includes all the furnishings." She pointedly omitted the fact that she had been at the mansion all morning with Pastor Bob.

"Bobbi, you know we always discuss important matters like this. I'm just shocked that you went ahead and did this without consulting me." Terry's voice was kind but firm.

"Terry, there just wasn't time. The asking price was so ridiculously low that I was afraid someone else would snap it up before we could make an offer. So I secured the contract with Mr. Van Cleve with a check for $50,000. Oh, Terry, this is like a dream come true. You know how I've wanted that place for years."

Terry loved Bobbi so much and would do anything to make her happy, but this was over the top. He almost lost control and yelled out, *"I can't believe you did this!"*

The other diners looked up when they heard Pastor Terry shout. He leaned across the table, looked Bobbi straight in the eyes, and said, "Come on, Bobbi! Let's go home and talk this over in private." They made a hasty retreat and left the other patrons wondering what was going on!

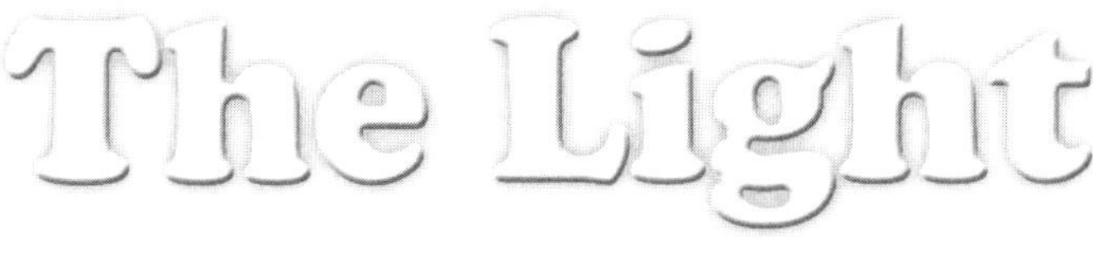

The halls of Centerville High School were abuzz with excitement! They had a championship boys' basketball team, and the campus had the feel of a winner!

The cafeteria was crowded and the air was alive with chatter and the sounds of horseplay.The members of the boys' basketball team sat together as a group and their girlfriends sat at a nearby table. After they finished lunch, they would pair off and stroll around the campus or just sit and talk somewhere.

Josh, Bobbi and Pastor Terry's handsome son, was a star basketball player and a very popular student. He ate exactly the same thing every day: three large slices of pepperoni pizza, a coke, and a couple of cookies for dessert. His girlfriend, Susie, was waiting for him to finish eating lunch so they could have a little time together before the next class. She caught his eye and he winked at her, indicating he was almost finished.

"Josh, have you *seen her?"* Josh's friend Ryan nudged him.

"Seen who? Who're you talking about?" All the guys at the table watched Josh to see his reaction. But he was merely confused.

"*Who?* Only the most beautiful girl God ever made! She's not a ten—she's more like a thousand. Wait till you see her. You'll think you've died and gone straight to heaven."

Josh knew how his friends overreacted to pretty girls, so he just grinned. He and Susie had been "together" since fifth grade and he was happy with her.

"Where did you see this goddess?" Josh teased his friend.

"Well, I happened to get a glimpse of her filling out papers in the office this morning. And I'm not kidding you, she really is *perfect."*

Some of the fellows shuffled their feet and poked each other under the table.

"Here she comes! Oh, be still my heart!"

"I think I'm going to faint!"

"Shut up, you guys! You're acting like idiots."

"Yeah, you're embarrassing me."

All sorts of comments could be heard around the table as their heads turned toward the door. Josh slowly turned his head, as well, and could almost feel every head in the cafeteria turn to watch the gorgeous, graceful blonde walk in.

"Well," Josh thought, "this time Ryan isn't exaggerating. That girl *is hot!"* He instantly felt disloyal to Susie, but he was enchanted.

The cafeteria was silent as the girl strolled directly to the players' table. The guys fidgeted but didn't say anything.

"Excuse me, I'm Lisa and I'm new. I hate to interrupt you, but I really do need some help figuring out how to get my lunch and then find Room 204." She was looking straight at Josh.

The girls at the adjoining table were watching this performance with amusement.

"Poor little thing—she can't figure out how to get her lunch."

"Yeah, *right!"*

"Come on, guys, close your mouths. You're making fools of yourselves."

The boys couldn't hear the comments but they knew they were being talked about.

Susie was especially attentive because it was obvious that this ravishing creature was looking right at her boyfriend.

Ryan kicked Josh hard under the table to get him out of his trance. It worked. Josh responded right away.

"Nice to meet you, Lisa. Come with me and I'll show you the ropes here. After you eat, I'll show you Room 204—my next class is there."

As the two walked toward the counter, the rest of the team rolled their eyes, pretended to fall off the bench, and made all sorts of ridiculous gestures of "appreciation of beauty."

Lisa looked up at Josh and asked him his name. He was so overwhelmed with her beauty and her attention he could hardly squeeze out the words, "My name is Josh, Josh Murphy."

Josh was usually confident and self-assured, but he felt flustered. "You can have hot lunches, sandwiches, or pizza," he said hurriedly.

"What do you usually have?" Lisa was a bit obvious in her attempt to charm Josh but he didn't notice. He just grinned from ear to ear and answered, "Pizza."

"Then I'll have pizza, too."

"I'll get it for you, Lisa. Sit down and I'll bring it right over."

As Josh fumbled for money to pay for the pizza, Susie stared in disbelief. What was Josh doing? All the other girls had gone off with their boyfriends and she was just sitting there, feeling foolish and getting angry. What was she supposed to do while Josh sat there with the beauty queen? She slowly rose from the table and went outside—glad that she knew how to pray and could ask Jesus how to react to all this.

The bell rang signaling the return to class, and Josh carried Lisa's books to Room 204. She promptly sat down next to him and made herself at home, seeming a bit more poised than the typical teenage girl.

Mr. Russell, the English teacher, introduced Lisa, as he did all new students, and she obviously relished the eyes that turned toward her. The tilt of her head and her body language invited attention.

After class Josh and Lisa chatted for a few minutes and he found out, to his amazement, that her schedule was identical to his. So they went to the next two classes together and after school was over, he asked if she needed a ride home.

"Well, I do need a ride, Josh, but I thought you had practice."

Within a few short hours, Josh's priorities had been knocked topsy-turvy. Josh shrugged, looked down at what he now considered the greatest thing to ever come into his life, and retorted, "Don't worry about it! Missing one day can't hurt that much. Anyway, I'm thirsty—we could stop for a coke, if you want to."

Lisa was practically purring at him as she walked beside him to his car. Almost everybody in the school saw what was going on and most of the guys were drooling with envy. Susie knew, too, and she felt her whole world collapsing. She couldn't figure out what was happening.

Lisa knew *exactly* what was happening. She was an integral part of an elaborate, wicked scheme and she was efficiently setting the trap for Josh Murphy.

"Josh," Lisa said, honey dripping from her voice, "my mother was talking to some friends about the Tyndall mansion outside of town and I've always wanted to see it. They made it sound like the most fabulous place in the world. Would it be too much trouble for us to drive out there and look at it?"

Josh's defenses were down so low that he didn't hesitate. They stopped for a coke at the Cline Vick Drugstore on the way out of town and made their way up the winding road. Josh had no way of knowing that he was the second Murphy to make the trek that day.

They passed the tennis courts and stables on the drive up to the fountain in front of the stately manor. Lisa seemed overwhelmed and exclaimed, "Josh, it's amazing! Have you ever seen anything so beautiful?"

"No, I sure haven't," Josh replied. But he wasn't referring to the mansion.

"Do you think they'd mind if we got out and walked around the grounds?"

"Can't do anything but throw us out if they catch us. Let's go."

After they'd walked around the yard a bit, Lisa playfully skipped up to the front door. She turned the doorknob and pretended to be surprised when it opened. Josh truly was surprised, because he didn't know everything had been planned by Lana. Lisa was merely following orders.

Like all curious teenagers, they entered the mansion and looked around. Lisa made appreciative noises like "Ooh and ah" before exclaiming. "Oh, Josh! Wouldn't you just love to live in a place like this? I would absolutely adore living here."

They wandered around inside the house a little more before going down by the lake. They sat down on the steps of the gazebo and drank in the cool air. Lisa was working her magic and Josh had no idea he was being manipulated by such an experienced expert.

"Josh, isn't this incredible? We could have some awesome parties up here, couldn't we? They've got everything: tennis courts, basketball courts, swimming pool, the lake and boats. Wonder who owns this place? It's obviously for sale." Lisa rattled on and on but all Josh could concentrate on was *her.*

Josh just kinda nodded as Lisa continued, "Thanks so much for bringing me up here. You've been so cool. I'd love to give you something in return."

As she spoke, she removed an expensive-looking necklace that had a gold dragon with ruby eyes hanging on a lavish gold chain. Josh thought the ruby eyes were looking right at him, and he felt almost hypnotized. Little did he know that Lana had prepared this necklace just for him.

"Josh, let me put the necklace on you; do you mind?"

Josh was enjoying all the attention and he was so captivated by Lisa that he would have done anything in the world to please her.

She put the necklace around Josh's neck and gently kissed his cheek as she secured the clasp. "Promise me you'll never take it off," she whispered. Josh felt a slight sense of danger, but he brushed it off, much like his mother had turned from the tiny whisper of caution earlier in the day. He didn't know what was happening here, but it was so good that he didn't want to mess it up.

As Lisa finished putting the necklace on Josh, he turned toward her and their eyes met. She quickly grabbed him and kissed him and from that point on, it was all over for Josh Murphy. He was completely in her control! Lisa was the only thing in the world that mattered to Josh—the trap had been set and Lana had used the perfect bait.

Josh and Lisa were just getting into their car to go back to town when Byron Van Cleve pulled up in his car.

"Josh, what a surprise to see you! I guess your mother told you she just bought this place. You're a lucky guy! I just drove up to take down the 'For Sale' sign and had no idea you'd already be up here. Save me a trip and take the key home to your mom, will you?"

Josh's mouth dropped open and he blurted, "What? I'm sorry, Mr. Van Cleve, but I have no idea what you're talking about!" He didn't mean to sound rude, but he really couldn't figure out what the man was saying.

Byron laughed. "No, Josh, I'm serious. Your mom put a deposit on this house this morning in my office. We're going to close the deal in about a week and you'll probably be moving in by the end of the next week."

Josh just looked at Lisa, who grabbed him and gave him a big hug. "Josh, this is absolutely awesome! How lucky can you get!"

By the look on Josh's face, he was completely baffled. So much had happened to him in the last few hours that he felt like he was on another planet. First Lisa, now this! Wait till he told Susie.

Susie! For the first time since he left school, Josh thought of Susie. Sweet, steady, loyal Susie. What must she be thinking right now? It was too much for Josh to ponder, so he just shoved her out of his mind and concentrated on "things" at hand. He felt Lisa take his hand and lean even closer to him. "Josh, we're going to have so much fun up here. I *will* be coming up here a lot with you, won't I?"

"Are you kidding, Lisa? Having you with me up here would make me the happiest guy on the planet." Josh had been completely swept off his feet that afternoon.

Even though Josh was filled with a jumble of emotions, he said very little on the drive back to town. His mind was racing and he couldn't grasp all that was happening.

As they jumped out of the car, Lisa told Josh she would call him but he hardly heard her. He could hardly wait to get home and see what was going on with the old mansion.

Entering the front door, Josh heard his parents' voices in the family room. Dashing into the room, beating his chest, and making a Tarzan-like noise, he yelled, "Mom! Dad! You've just made me the happiest guy in the whole world! I saw Mr. Van Cleve and he told me about the Tyndall mansion. Did someone die and leave us a fortune? How can we afford that place?" The words came tumbling out!

"Josh, come on in, son. I'm glad you're here. Your mom and I have just been discussing it and we still have some things to iron out. I'm not even sure I understand exactly what took place this morning, although she's been trying to explain it to me."

Bobbi jumped in, "Honey, I told you all there is to know. Those visitors in church yesterday morning gave a total of $200,000 in the offering and the Tyndall mansion is on the market for exactly $200,000! Personally, I think that's a miracle! You know I've always dreamed of living up there. This must be God's way of answering my prayer."

Terry remained silent and Bobbi looked to him for affirmation. However, she got none, but his unresponsiveness didn't dampen her enthusiasm one bit.

"Terry, you know I'm right! When I found out the house was for sale, I knew right away that we should get it. I'm sure! I'm so sure!"

Josh was looking back and forth at his parents, feeling more confused than ever. "Maybe we aren't really going to get the old house," he thought. "What would Lisa think of me then?"

Terry's voice broke into Josh's reverie. "Josh, this isn't really a done deal yet, so don't go telling any of your friends. I've got to call a board meeting this evening and get some wisdom on this whole thing." Looking at Bobbi, he continued, "After all, this is *church money,* you know. We can't just take offerings and spend them without the church board's knowledge. We can't be involved in anything dishonest—or even questionable."

Bobbi suddenly looked tense and upset, much as she had on the drive back to town when she and Terry had taken JJ and Lynn up to see the mansion. However, she remained quiet because she didn't want her son to see her throw a tantrum.

Even though she mentally tuned Terry out, she could still hear his voice in the background. He had a habit of verbalizing what he was going to do—sort of an audible organizer—and she had learned not to let it bother her.

"Uncle Pete called to let me know he's feeling fine after his tests, ready to get back to work, so I'll have him set up the meeting for eight o'clock. I was just thinking that it might be a good idea if we ran back up to the mansion and looked at it one more time. It would probably be a good idea if I got more details so I can give the board an intelligent overview of what it offers."

Bobbi quickly snapped out of her "pout" as she heard the last part of what Terry said. "You mean you want to go back up to look at it *now?* Josh, do you want to come? Maybe JJ and Lynn would like to ride up with us, too. I know they wanted to be left alone to write but this calls for a celebration! I'm sure they'll come. Josh, will you call them for me?"

JJ and Lynn declined the invitation but assured them that they wanted to hear all the details later.

Bobbi could sense a subtle shift in Terry's mood. "Maybe he's warming to the idea of living in a mansion," she thought.

On the ride up, Josh told his parents all about Lisa and how she had burst into his life that day. His parents didn't interrupt his excited story, but they exchanged glances several times as he babbled on—a most uncharacteristic display for him.

His mother couldn't stand it any longer, "But, Josh! What about Susie? You and Susie have been best friends for years and we always assumed..." Bobbi wisely dropped her voice and let the assumption hang in the air. Everyone knew what she was going to say and it would be better left unsaid.

"I know, Mom." Josh sounded odd. "I guess everybody thought the same thing—I know I did, too. *But Lisa!* Wait till you meet her! She's *awesome!* I never dreamed I'd find somebody like her. You'll understand when you meet her—and Susie will just have to understand, too, I guess. But I guess I'd better talk to her, huh?"

"Speaking of Susie," Terry interrupted, "I've been meaning to tell you both about what happened. She gave me a little booklet that JJ had given her and it explained all about being 'born again' and getting closer to God. It happens when you make a deliberate decision to believe that Jesus died for your sins, and repent. When you do that, the Spirit of God enters you—it's a miracle! Susie said she had done it, too."

Josh exclaimed, "You know, I guess I *had* noticed something different about Susie. In fact, she kept saying all weekend that she wanted to tell me something exciting and we were supposed to talk right after lunch, but then I got distracted...maybe that's what she wanted to talk to me about. She must think I'm a real jerk! What did she tell you, Dad?"

"Susie was so happy that she glowed and when she gave me the pamphlet, she was so excited that I promised her I'd read it even before I knew what it was. But after I repeated the prayer at the end of the booklet and felt His presence come into me, I understood what a powerful experience she had had. Because I had it, too! Now I want to read the Bible and talk to Him all the time. This is the most wonderful thing that's ever happened to me."

"Well, Dad, the most exciting and wonderful thing that's happened to me lately is meeting Lisa!"

"And the most exciting and wonderful thing that's happened to me involves this mansion. Maybe we can discuss all this other stuff later." Bobbi was direct! Then she thought of Pastor Bob and what had happened earlier in the day and her face burned.

"By the way, Honey, I forgot to tell you that I picked up some paperwork on the house and it probably has all the information you'd need for your presentation to the Board tonight. Stuff about yearly taxes and any kind of encumbrances on the property. But it's still good for you to look around, I guess. Come on, let's go."

"Well, that'll help. But I wish you had thought of those things before you wrote that check to Byron." Terry was still smarting from the knowledge that his wife had made such a major decision without consulting him—and the church Board.

Josh was impatient! "Come on! Let's see what you came to see, Dad, then I need to get home. Lisa might call."

Their stay was short. Bobbi had seen all she needed to see when she toured the mansion with Pastor Bob (although no one else knew that), Josh had been all over the place with Lisa that afternoon, and Pastor Terry had his written data, so they were all satisfied when they left.

They stopped by the cottage to share their excitement with JJ and Lynn, who tried to act happy, but they both felt apprehensive as they listened. Terry and his family stayed only a few minutes and JJ and Lynn were glad they didn't have to discuss the mansion further.

"JJ, this mansion thing is not all it appears to be. It's exactly like this town: everything looks good on the surface but evil lurks in every corner." Lynn voiced her concern.

"You're absolutely right about that, Honey. I'm so glad we're able to work in this cottage because it hasn't been touched by that evil. My dad used to live here, you know, and he was such a wonderful man of God. I believe that a special anointing of God still resides here because of him."

"Maybe that's why the book is coming together so well, JJ. If we keep going at this pace, we'll have it done in a couple of weeks."

"Honey, it's so great to have you helping me on this project. I know this book is going to do major damage to Satan and his kingdom and we need to stand together to see it to completion. This cottage is a real godsend."

Lynn was quick to agree. "Do you think it'll be difficult to find a publisher once we're finished?"

JJ was always so calm and steady. Through the years Lynn had come to rely on that many times. "Nah, we won't have any trouble getting this book published. God is in this and He'll not only find us a good publisher but He'll also get it promoted. We aren't to worry about any of that." It was as simple as that for him—and he conveyed that confidence to his wife.

While JJ and Lynn worked on their book throughout the evening, Pastor Terry was at the church skillfully presenting his proposal to the Board.

"This is an extraordinary opportunity for us to wisely invest the large amount of money that was contributed on Sunday morning."

He went on to expound on the exceptional value of the property. "Why, even the land itself is worth more than they're asking for the mansion and all the furnishings. And there's a tennis court, a basketball court, stables, swimming pool, a lake. The possibilities for youth activities—well, just think about it!"

They were convinced! Pastor Terry was quite a persuasive man. And some of the Board members wanted Pastor Terry to be sure to tell Bobbi what a good job she had done in showing such initiative and skill in grabbing up the property before anyone else got to it.

Bobbi was waiting up for Terry when he got home and insisted on hearing every detail of the meeting. When he told her that some of the Board members had complimented her, she felt smug, but she hid it under a facade of pleasantness and sweetness. She realized there was quite a bit she didn't want her husband to know these days, so she'd better learn to mask her feelings.

The Light

11

Bobbi was up early the next morning sorting and packing. Even Josh bounded downstairs earlier than usual, gave his mom a quick hug, and said he had to get to school early.

When Bobbi asked him why he was going to school so early, Josh replied, "Gotta catch up on some stuff." Actually, he was hoping to see Lisa before classes started—why did he feel the need to keep that information from his mother?

"Okay, Son. By the way, it's okay to tell you friends about the mansion, because the Board approved everything last night."

"Oh, Mom, I may tell some of the guys, but *I'll sure tell Lisa.* She's gonna love this." He was so relieved.

Pastor Terry was out of the house early, as well, for a breakfast meeting, so Bobbi was alone in the house, humming as she cleaned out storage spaces. She was having the time of her life! When the phone rang, she answered brightly, "Good morning!"

"Good morning, Bobbi. This is Bob. I just heard the good news and wondered if we could meet for lunch and celebrate—my treat! How about The Lamplighter around noon?"

Bobbi was unexpectedly happy to hear his voice, but hesitated before answering, "Well, Bob, I don't know. Isn't there some place a little less conspicuous?"

Perfect! Pastor Bob was silent for a moment, then replied, "There is a place that's ideal but it's quite a little drive. Have you ever been to the Gold Mine Restaurant?"

"Yes, and I love it!" Bobbi heard her voice acquiescing, against her better judgment.

"Then, let's go! If you can drive out to the old furniture store on the edge of town, I think it used to be Cox's Furniture before it was abandoned, I'll meet you there. We can drive up in my car."

"That works for me. What time, Bob?"

"Let's meet at eleven o'clock so we won't have to rush." Lowering his voice, Pastor Bob added, "I can't wait to see you, Bobbi."

Bobbi called Terry's office and left a message with his secretary, giving a fictitious excuse for being away from the house part of the day.

Pastor Bob immediately called Lana. "Lana? Pastor Bob. Bobbi and I are meeting at the abandoned furniture store outside of town, then driving up to the Gold Mine Restaurant for lunch, so make sure somebody sees us. And make sure someone gets pictures, too."

Lana hated even the hint of someone telling her what to do, so she interrupted him, speaking firmly, "I'm on top of the situation!" Her voice was shrill. "Stay where you are and I'll be there in a few minutes with my latest brew of potion. Be sure you stop for coffee on the way up so you can dump it in her cup. This is it!" Her voice took on the sound of triumph. "This is it! Pastor, it's time to move in for the kill. I'm counting on you to work your magic!" She hung up the phone and her voice vibrated with evil glee. She hurried to Pastor Bob's place, carrying her precious cargo: love potion.

Pastor Bob was energized. He relished the intrigue and complicity, and, to be totally honest, he was anticipating his assignment because he was strongly attracted to Bobbi. She was dazzling, smart, and vulnerable and seemed to be responding to him. She was fair game for seduction—and he definitely was a seducer! Not slick and smarmy, but sophisticated, intelligent and seemingly sincere. And far too handsome for his own good. To many women he was irresistible—and he expected the same to be true of this woman.

Pastor Bob and Bobbi met at their pre-arranged rendezvous. She got into his car and they were both too preoccupied with greeting each other to notice the car that passed by, slowing as the driver recognized the two occupants. At Bob's suggestion, they got a cup of coffee at a drive-through window before they got out of town. Bob's "drop" was easily accomplished and he knew the potion would be in effect before they reached their destination.

Frank Moore, Chairman of the Board of Centerville Christian Center, had met with Byron Van Cleve the day before to discuss a loan. This morning Byron had called to inquire if he would like to meet him for lunch to further discuss the loan. Byron then told him that he had business with the owner of Gold Mine Restaurant and if Frank had time, he'd like for them to have lunch there. In that way, Byron could kill two birds with one stone.

Frank was flattered that one of The Big Three in town would invite him to drive out of town for lunch. He had picked up Byron at the bank and offered to drive, and Byron assented. What difference did it make to him? He was just going along with the plan.

"Frank, I heard this morning that your pastor is buying the old Tyndall mansion."

"That's right! What a steal! The land alone is worth more than what they're asking for the whole bundle."

"You're right about that," agreed Byron. "It's the buy of the century!"

Byron had suggested that they stop for a cup of coffee because he wanted to be sure Pastor Bob and Bobbi arrived at the restaurant before they did, as Lana had instructed.

Arriving at the restaurant, Pastor Bob requested a window seat toward the back of the room. He wanted it to appear to Bobbi that he wanted privacy, yet he knew they had to be in an area where they could be seen by other diners (especially Frank and Byron).

Pastor Bob and Bobbi were enjoying a delicious lunch when Frank and Byron walked in, and Byron made it a point to seat Frank where he would have a clear view of the couple. Pastor Bob made sure that he kept Bobbi's full attention so she wouldn't notice that they were being watched. Things were going according to plan!

"Isn't that your pastor's wife over there with the pastor from the other church?" Byron feigned surprise.

"Where?" Frank looked up from his menu and gasped in amazement. Bobbi seemed totally engrossed in conversation and had no idea she was being watched, but Frank felt a little queasy in the pit of his stomach. "What could she possibly be doing way up here with Pastor Bob?" he wondered.

Bobbi sat back in her chair and put her hand to her face. "I feel a little flushed from the coffee. I guess I drank it too fast because it made me feel warm all over. In fact, I feel a little strange."

Pastor Bob solicitously reached for her hand. "Don't worry, you'll be all right. Maybe it had too much sugar in it." He pulled her hand toward him and kissed her fingertips. Bobbi's heart raced and she stifled an overwhelming impulse to kiss his hand, as well. Bobbi gazed at Pastor Bob with a longing look in her eyes, and Pastor Bob knew she was close to being overcome with emotion. He hoped the "emotion" was yearning for him.

"I've got to have Lana give me some of this stuff," he thought. "I knew I was good at seduction but this stuff works better than anything I can do."

Bobbi could no longer resist! Continuing to look deep into Pastor Bob's eyes, she lifted his hand, caressed it slowly, then returned the kiss. She could hardly believe what she was doing—but she continued to hold his hand! And her eyes never left his. She was completely oblivious to their surroundings.

Byron and Frank witnessed the entire scene! Frank became so outraged that he excused himself from his table and marched over to where Bob and Bobbi were sitting.

"Mrs. Murphy! Pastor Bob! Imagine running into you two here!" Frank's voice was jovial and affable, and he had no intention of creating a scene, but his eyes flashed anger. "Mrs. Murphy, I feel I have to ask: Is this a regular thing? Has this been going on long? Does Pastor Terry know about you?"

Bobbi pulled away from Pastor Bob, shocked and humiliated. She started to speak, but Pastor Bob hurriedly took command.

"Now just a minute, Frank. Be careful what you say. Mrs. Murphy deserves your respect and I'm not going to allow anyone to speak to her like that in my presence."

Bobbi was so stunned and upset that she stood up and reached for her sweater. "Come on, Bob, let's get out of here!"

Pastor Bob paid the check and followed her out the door.The sound of slamming doors and screeching tires could be heard inside the restaurant as they sped away.

Frank knew he should have tempered his approach a bit, but he was so unprepared for what he saw that he forgot all about social graces. He didn't think anything else could shock him that day, but Byron delivered another bombshell as soon as he sat down.

"Frank, I've just been wondering about something, and figured you would know, since you're the Chairman of the Board over at that church. How can the church get away with taking $200,000 that was designated for something else and use it to buy a house for the pastor?"

Frank's face grew red and he looked like he was going to explode. "*What?* What are you talking about?" He was yelling and calling attention to himself. "Anyway, how do you know so much about what our church does with its money?"

"I work at the bank, remember? Because of the large amounts of some of the checks, a teller asked me to look them over. I noticed that they were all earmarked for the missions fund but Bobbi Murphy wrote me a large check later in the day from that same account. Isn't there something illegal about buying a mansion with church funds?"

The Light

12

Susie fought tears all the way over to the cottage where JJ and Lynn were still working on their book. She had been able to keep her emotions in check at school and at work (how else would she get good tips?) but now that her shift was over, she felt like she was going to lose it. She needed to talk to someone! She was confused and angry and crushed and she couldn't figure it out. It seemed like ever since she accepted Jesus, her whole life had gone downhill.

"Susie, what a nice surprise!" Lynn greeted the teen like a long-lost friend. "I'm so glad to see you! Come on in—are you here to study the Bible some more?"

Susie barely got inside the door when she burst into tears. Lynn instinctively put her arm around the girl's shoulders and steered her toward the couch.

"Lynn, I can't believe what's happened. My whole life's falling apart. I can't figure out why God is letting this happen to me." Susie was still crying but she was coherent.

"Josh—your own nephew—has been my boyfriend since fifth grade and we made all these promises to each other. We go everywhere together and we know each other better than anyone else in the world. We vowed that nothing would ever separate us, but something sure has. I just can't figure it all out—something really weird is going on."

Lynn interrupted Susie and offered her a soft drink. "There, I'm glad you've calmed down a little, Susie. Now tell me the rest of the story. What do you mean by weird?"

"I'm sure you know that Josh is the center for the basketball team and no one else can take his place. Centerville has a good chance of taking the state championship this year, but not if Josh quits. It's so stupid! He went up to Coach Doug today and told him that if he had to take off his necklace, he wouldn't play anymore. A necklace! I don't even know where he got that ugly thing—it's new—and it looks spooky. What makes it stranger is that Josh has been *living* for his senior year and this championship. It's all he could talk about last year."

Susie stopped to take a breath and a sip of her drink. "And the other thing is, this new girl Lisa! Josh dumped me for her! In *one day* he gets all wrapped up in the type of girl that he always said he didn't admire. Her clothes are so tight that she looks like she's been poured into them. I have to admit she's really beautiful, though. It's hard not to be jealous of her, Lynn, even though I know it's not right. But now that I think of it, maybe Lisa gave that necklace to Josh, because he doesn't own any type of jewelry. He always said he hates to wear jewelry—it gets in his way. I'll bet that's it—Lisa gave him that necklace and made him promise not to take it off."

Lynn looked like a light had just been turned on in her head and she exclaimed, "I'll bet that's it! I'll guarantee that's what happened! JJ, can you come in here?"

Susie had no idea what Lynn was talking about, but she trusted her. JJ joined them quickly and Lynn continued, "JJ, it sounds like Josh has had a spell or hex put on him. This could be very serious."

JJ nodded in agreement, "I think you're right, Honey!"

They both saw the look of bewilderment on Susie's face and Lynn paused to explain, "Susie, do you remember when you turned your life over to Jesus? We prayed that day that all the demons would be removed from your life. We kick out all the evil, demonic influences and it makes Satan and his kingdom very upset. They immediately set up a plan of action to try to get back into your life and take control. But we're not going to let that happen. We know Satan's tactics and how he works and we're going to pray, and agree, and break his plan right now!"

"Could I stay and pray with you, Reverend Murphy?"

"Absolutely! And, Susie, it's okay if you call me JJ."

Susie beamed! "Thanks, JJ."

"This is a good time for you to learn to do warfare and keep Satan out of your life," Lynn said, taking Susie's hand.

The three of them prayed for about twenty minutes and JJ spoke up, "Susie, I really feel that we should pray over Josh. Do you think you could contact him and bring him over here about this time tomorrow?"

"I'll do my best, JJ. It will probably be a challenge to get him away from Lisa, though. Pray for me."

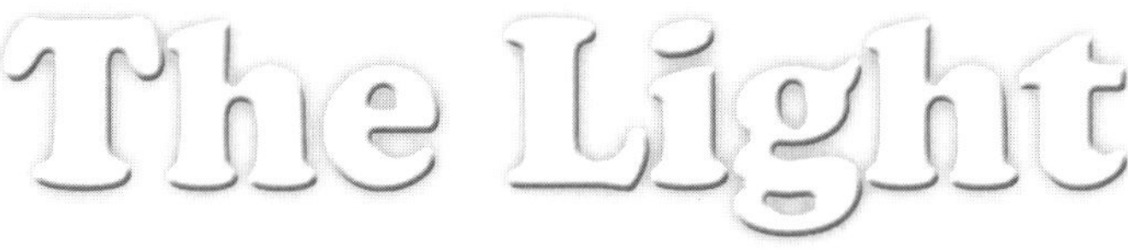

The Light

13

Up on the hill in the massive study of Mayor Casey's mansion, Lana and her contingent of evildoers were savoring a dinner of celebration. Joining them were the beautiful Lisa and The Big Three from downtown. Toward the end of the meal, someone put on a CD and got up to dance. After all, this was a victory dinner!

Lana's deep red lips were smiling but her depraved, evil face stayed tight. When she could stand it no longer, she screamed, "Listen up! Everybody's finished eating, so let's have some VICTORY TALK! Victory! I love the word. We have won the war, comrades, and all we have to do now is sit back and watch the sparks fly. And we've really set some pretty hot sparks! You have all performed magnificently, so you can plan to go home tomorrow—at least most of you can. Lisa, of course, will be staying and I don't mind if you stay with your daughter, Darlene. She still has a little bit left on her assignment and it would look odd for her to be in town without family."

Lisa was pleased because she was enjoying what she was doing. And she was surprised that everything had come together so quickly, so flawlessly.

"Congratulations, Pastor Bob! You, too, Lisa! You two sure know how to use that spirit of lust—but always remember that your power comes from our esteemed Leader. If you ever cross him, you'll find yourselves crumpled in a heap somewhere."

"Because of you two, Pastor Terry's household is in shambles. His wife is totally smitten with a new man and Lisa has complete control over his son. This has all happened so quickly that he's not even aware of the scope of it. But the biggest shock for him is going to come when he gets arrested for fraud." Lana actually smacked her lips in delight.

"Mayor Casey, start working on getting formal charges made against Pastor Terry and his church. Include all the Board members, because they approved the purchase of the mansion." Mayor Casey started taking notes and it was obvious that he was eager to get started.

Lana was eager, too. "I can't wait! Once they get that preacher locked up, Centerville will be ours again!"

Byron knew he was next—and he was right. "Byron, spread the word that the plans for the new housing development on the north side of town fell through. Give them any reason you want —lack of interest, lack of funding, whatever. You're smart—you know what to do." Byron nodded assent. He liked the compliment.

"Well, you've all done a great job! Very impressive! Now we can all just sit back and relax a little. Don't let your guard down too far, but most of the preliminary work is done. Now we can just watch the fallout. I have to go to Washington, D.C. for a couple of days to take care of minor problems. Apparently a few stupid humans with the light in them are trying to mess up our Leader's plans there."

Lana just had another realization! "Oh, just one more thing. When we get rid of Pastor Terry, we'll also get rid of that stupid uncle and aunt of his. They really need to get out of town because I haven't been able to implement a fatal accident for them. They're just too full of *the light* and they constantly bind up our powers." Even an inkling of failure threw Lana into fits of rage, but she felt victory knocking on the door!

"Drink up! Dance! Celebrate! We've won, comrades! We've won!" Her voice rang out "we" but inside she was thinking, "*I won!* Now our Leader will reward me with more power."

The Light

14

Frank had lost no time calling his friends on the Board and reporting what he had witnessed at the Gold Mine Restaurant. He was sickened and horrified and felt he couldn't carry the burden of the knowledge by himself. He wasn't being gossipy—he just needed to share and try to get some wisdom on how they should proceed.

Although all the Board members were equally shocked and alarmed, none of them wanted to expose the situation or confront the pastor. They deeply loved and highly respected him, so they agreed to just "sit on" the information and see what happened.

Pastor Terry was on the phone early the next morning, summoning all the Board members to The

Lamplighter for an impromptu, but urgent, breakfast meeting.

The members of the Board gathered at the big, round table usually occupied by The Big Three, but they were already out golfing, so they wouldn't be showing up.

Pastor Terry wasn't at the restaurant when the last of the Board members arrived, so they freely discussed matters among themselves. Was Pastor Terry going to discuss the secret meetings his wife was having with Pastor Bob? Was he going to further discuss the proposed purchase of the old mansion? Neither subject made them feel very comfortable--but nothing could have prepared them for the shocking news Pastor Terry shared when he arrived. They had expected him to appear somber when he walked in, but he looked absolutely ebullient.

"Good morning, gentlemen! Sorry to get you out so early this morning, but I've been so tied up and preoccupied that I haven't been able to share some great news with you. My life has been completely changed and it wouldn't be right for me to keep it from you any longer."

What could Pastor Terry possibly be talking about? The waitress took their orders, then their pastor continued.

"I came into some truth that utterly contradicts much of what I have been preaching these last few years. Since you comprise the leadership of the church, I felt I should share with you before I tell the entire congregation."

The men were waiting!

"A few days ago, right here in this restaurant, a young lady whom you all know gave me a booklet which I promised to read. It explained all about Jesus Christ and how He came to earth to die for our sins, then rose again and returned to heaven. I've known that story, but I never believed that I needed to accept Jesus as my personal Lord and Savior. Well, I do now! In fact, I accepted Him just a few nights ago and the moment I believed, I felt this big load lift off my shoulders."

The men sitting around the table shifted uncomfortably in their seats and exchanged puzzled looks. Pastor Terry was so caught up in his testimony that he was unaware of any of this.

"I am so free! All I want to do is read the Bible and spend time with Him in prayer—and tell everyone I know what has happened to me. But I needed to tell you first, because my sermons are going to radically change! People may come up to you and ask what's happened to me."

"But, Pastor Terry, you and your father always told us that Jesus was just a great prophet who taught us to obey the laws of the land and be kind to our neighbors. Does this mean you've changed your mind?"

"Yes, that's exactly what it means. I've misled you in the past but now that I've discovered the truth, I *must* set things right. I was wrong, totally wrong, and I am so sorry. That's the bad news. The good news is that you can all be changed, too, if you will just believe! I've rediscovered the Bible and I'm convinced that we will live forever, either in heaven or hell, and the choice is ours. I know! I've been telling you there is no hell, but friends, I've been wrong. Please hear me out. I am trying to correct my error and let you know that if any one of you here right now believes what I'm telling you, you can accept Jesus into your heart. All you have to do is repeat a prayer after me—and believe it as you pray."

This was an amazing new pastor sitting with them this morning. Without exception, each man felt an unfamiliar stirring in his heart that made him want to believe his story and respond to the truth. They felt deep loyalty for Pastor Terry because he had been a great leader since his father and mother died in a car accident.

The Board members remained silent. They seemed to sense their unity and almost simultaneously nodded assent. Yes, they all wanted to pray that prayer, even the crustiest, most cantankerous one among them. No one was arguing this morning.

Pastor Terry led them in a prayer asking God to forgive them and take control of their lives. Tears were streaming down many faces when they finished and the waitress was reluctant to approach the table with their orders. She had been listening as she lingered in the background and she was deeply moved by the change in the men's appearance. However, she knew what had just taken place.

"Pastor Terry!" the waitress whispered, "forgive me, but I couldn't help overhearing your prayer and I have to share with you that I prayed that same prayer just last night. Susie gave all the workers here these little booklets and by what I've heard already this morning, a lot of us repeated the prayer. Everyone who comes in to work is so excited, I'm not sure we're going to get much work done today. We all want to come to your church on Sunday!"

Such music for a pastor's heart! Even the Board members were overwhelmed with emotion. The Chairman of the Board spoke up. "This is absolutely wonderful!"

"Is that all the business, Pastor Terry? I really want to get home and tell my wife what's just happened!"

"That's it, gentlemen. Enjoy your day! Spread the word! And I'll see you all again soon."

There was much gulping of coffee as they gathered up their belongings, stuffed some extra donuts and rolls in napkins, and threw some bills on the table. They left at pretty much the same, excitedly comparing notes on what had just transpired, apparently forgetting all about the old mansion and the reports about Pastor Bob and Bobbi.

The Light

15

It was the last class of the day and Lisa was ready to bolt out of her seat. She had plans that didn't include Josh but she knew she had to give him some sort of explanation. She certainly couldn't tell him that Lana had given her a couple of days off, so she didn't have to work on her "assignment" during that time. She planned to lie in the sun at the luxurious home they were occupying during their time in Centerville, and she'd have time for a manicure. She had seen a shade of purple/black polish she wanted to try on her nails and who knows? She thought she might even get a toe ring. She was free to indulge whatever whim interested her.

"Josh, wait up!" Josh had been looking forward to "waiting up" to be with Lisa, as he did after every class.

"Sure—what's up?"

"Josh, I'm sorry we can't do anything today. I've got to help my mom with some things—but I'll see you first thing tomorrow, honest! I'll miss you terribly and I'll be thinking of you every minute. You're the most wonderful thing that ever happened to me." She was laying it on a little thick, but Josh didn't seem to notice. "Besides, won't you be helping your mom pack today? Well, gotta run. See you later!" And before Josh could respond to anything, she was gone.

Josh sat stunned for just a couple of minutes and was jarred back to awareness by Susie's voice.

"Josh, we really need to talk. Could you possibly give me a ride home?" Why did she feel so tentative? After all, he hadn't told her they were breaking up or anything. He'd just been *weird!*

"Sure. Let's go." Not much enthusiasm there!

"I'm supposed to stop by the cottage to see your uncle for a minute. Is that okay?"

"Sure," Josh answered again. "Don't you work today?"

"You know this is my day off—but I guess you forgot." He seemed to be forgetting a lot of things lately, she thought.

They walked slowly to his car and he didn't even open the door for her, which he always did. Neither of them spoke on the short drive over to the cottage.

Lynn heard their knock and hurriedly opened the door. "Come in, you two! Nice to see you, Josh. We knew Susie was coming so we got some pizza—and you're welcome to stay, of course." Lynn was so glad to see that Susie had been able to get Josh to their place.

One sure way to get Josh's attention was to mention pizza, and he followed them into the kitchen.

"Hi, Uncle JJ, I hear you need some help with your pizza!"

"Josh! Great to see you!" JJ gave him a hearty slap on the back, picked up the pizza, and guided him toward the screened porch.

"Lynn, will you and Susie bring out the drinks? Josh and I'll lay out the paper plates and napkins."

Turning his attention back to Josh, JJ said, "You must be awfully excited about moving. Have you been helping your mom pack?" He didn't know that Susie could overhear him.

"Move? Pack? What on earth are you talking about? Who's moving?" Susie got a pained expression on her face because she realized Josh hadn't been sharing with her—and it hurt.

Susie's mouth dropped open. "Josh, are you leaving Centerville?"

"Oh, nothing like that, Susie. I thought maybe you'd already heard. My folks just bought the old Tyndall mansion and we'll be moving in this weekend."

"Isn't that awfully quick?" Susie had helped move before and knew what a big job it was. "How can you afford the mansion? It must be worth over a million dollars. And, Josh, why didn't you tell me yourself?—we tell each other everything." Her voice wasn't accusing, just inquiring, although the pain was there.

"Yeah, Susie, I know, but I've been awfully busy lately," Josh replied sheepishly. "It's hard to explain but I'll give you the short version. Remember all those guests we had in church on Sunday? Well, they put $200,000 in the offering and that's the exact asking price of the mansion, so my mom put a deposit to seal the contract. The church Board approved it and they're going to sign the papers Friday and we're moving in Saturday. Pretty cool, huh?"

"Yes, it's real cool; in fact, it sounds like a miracle. But I still can't believe you didn't tell me."

JJ quickly interrupted Susie. He knew the two young people had some talking to do, but it would have to wait. Right now he felt an urgency to get down to some spiritual business.

"Who are these strangers who have come into town, Josh?"

"Well, Uncle JJ, all I know is that they came here to start a new housing development on the north side and the whole town is talking about it. And they must be pretty rich to put that kind of money in the offering."

"And who is the new girl in your school named Lisa?" asked Lynn.

Oh, oh. Now it was getting personal. Josh flushed and squirmed. "She's the daughter of Darlene, the architect for the project. It just happened that she is in all the exact classes I have and I've been helping her find her away around. After all, she's new."

Josh thought that was the end of it, but JJ pressed on. "Did she give you a necklace, Josh?"

Josh's hand instinctively went to his throat and he became a little defensive. "Well, yes, she did give me a necklace in return for a favor." What was going on here? This was getting a little out of hand, but Josh didn't want to be rude—and he didn't want to leave before all the favorite pizza was gone.

"Could I see the necklace, Josh?" JJ reached out his hand.

Pulling back a bit, Josh replied, "But, Uncle JJ, she made me promise never to take it off."

"It'll be okay, Josh."

As Josh reluctantly pulled the necklace from under his shirt, the ruby eyes began to glow. Everyone but Josh could see it—he was getting dizzy and his head fell to the back of the chair. As if in a trance, he said, "I have to go see Lisa right now. I have to go! I MUST GO! RIGHT NOW!" Then he drifted off, the necklace still around his neck.

Lynn was on her feet instantly and came back with a little vial of oil that they called "anointing oil."

"Thanks, Honey," JJ whispered.

"Susie, pray like you've never prayed before," instructed JJ. Then he poured some of the oil in his hands and began to pray.

"Lord, let this oil be a symbol of the blood of Jesus and the power of the Holy Spirit." Then he placed his hands, wet with oil, on the necklace and prayed further:

"In the Name of Jesus, I break the power of any curse, hex, or spell that is attached to this necklace in any way, shape or form. I cancel its assignment and command it to go back to the demon that brought it. I command that devil to go bound out to uninhabited dry places, bound with the living blood of Jesus Christ."

Suddenly Josh was jolted back to his senses and sat up, a dazed look on his face—but his eyes were clear.

"What happened?"

"Josh, there was a spell attached to the necklace Lisa gave you. You need to take it off immediately, then later I should explain what is happening."

Without hesitation, Josh removed the necklace and handed it to JJ. Then he looked at Susie—and she could tell *her* Josh was back.

"Susie! I'm sorry. Please forgive me for the way I've been acting. I've really not been myself lately." He wasn't making excuses—he really *hadn't* been himself lately, and now he realized it.

Susie smiled that brilliant smile, but there were tears in her eyes. "It's okay, Josh. I understand, but I'm glad you're yourself again."

"Uncle JJ, were you going to explain something to me?" asked Josh.

"Why don't you and Susie take a walk by the lake, Josh? It's obvious that you have things to talk about—I'll be here when you get back." He lovingly waved them off as emotion swept over him. He was startled at the depth of his love for this boy.

A couple of hours later Lynn and JJ smiled at each other as they saw Josh and Susie approaching the porch, hand in hand. This was good! JJ and Lynn had spent the entire time praying, and from the looks of things, it paid off.

Susie's beautiful smile was radiant and her eyes were dancing. "Josh prayed the prayer in the pamphlet, too! Isn't that wonderful?"

It truly was wonderful! One look at Josh's face confirmed the change that had taken place in him.

"Uncle JJ, my dad tried to tell us the other night about what had happened to him, but my mind was closed. Actually, my mind was on other things. I should've listened 'cuz I've never felt so free! I can't wait for the other kids to hear about it." Then he almost pounced on JJ as he exclaimed, "I just had a great idea! Why don't you and Aunt Lynn come over to the youth meeting tonight and share with everybody!"

Susie interrupted, "Josh, it's almost time for the meeting to start! We'd better get over there and get things set up."

"Can you come, Uncle JJ? Maybe we can talk some more since we still haven't had time for you to explain to me what happened here on the porch earlier."

Of course, JJ and Lynn were more than delighted to join them, and the four walked over to the church together. Several dozen young people had already gathered in anticipation of the evening's event. There was always a great turnout because Centerville Christian Center provided an abundance of assorted "junk" food and soft drinks. Purely a social affair, the youth ate well and enjoyed lots of activities such as Ping Pong, shooting hoops, and video games. It was designed to be a wholesome evening but there was no hint of Jesus being honored or even acknowledged.

Josh was the most popular boy in high school, so that boosted attendance—everyone loved to be around Josh. His persuasive powers could convince his friends to help with anything, and they were like busy bees setting up tables and preparing the food.

When it was time to start, Josh called for everybody to find a seat and be quiet. Standing up on the platform in front of everybody, he beamed, "Welcome! Glad to see everybody! We're going to have a great time tonight, as usual, but before we start eating and playing games, I've got some really exciting news to share with you and I'm going to give everybody a very important little booklet to read. It'll change your life! Then I'm going to introduce you to my Uncle JJ and he's going to spend a little time sharing, too."

Looking down at JJ, Josh asked, "Do you have some more of these pamphlets, Uncle JJ?"

JJ had to run back to the house and get a supply, so Josh and Susie began telling their friends what had happened to them. Susie had already told a lot of her classmates about her experience, but the anointing of the Holy Spirit was so strong on her that it sounded new and fresh.

When Josh began to speak, a hush fell over the audience and the atmosphere was charged with disbelief mingled with awe. This was not the Josh Murphy they knew. Yes, he was a great guy, charismatic and dynamic, but tonight he was different. There was a passion in his voice and eyes as he spoke they had never seen before. Not an eye left his face as he told them simply and directly that Jesus loved them, had died for their sins, and would give them eternal life if they would choose Him. Feelings swept over them that they had never felt before and tears began to flow.

When JJ returned with the tracts, he was greeted by this beautiful scene. With the help of some of the students, he quickly passed out a tract to each student.

Josh had the students follow along as he read vital parts of the pamphlet, then made a very clear-cut appeal. "I believe all of you understand what I'm about to ask you, so you can make the right decision. If you are really serious and want to be forgiven of your sins so that you can live your life for Jesus, repeat this prayer after me."

It looked to JJ and Lynn like every one of the seventy-five youth in the room that night prayed the prayer. They did not pray in hushed tones—they prayed loudly, boldly, and confidently. It was beautiful. Many tears flowed as they hugged each other, asked forgiveness from one another, and even laughed with joy. JJ saw a boy go up to another, reach in his pocket for some money, then give it to the other one. Repaying a debt, no doubt. The Holy Spirit was doing a quick work in hearts.

Regaining control of the crowd was a challenge, but Josh was able to get everyone settled down.

"Okay, guys, it looks to me like you've all been changed—and things are going to change around here. We've left Jesus completely out of our plans and meetings in the past, but now He is going to be the main focus. Your parents might not be prepared for this, so telling them should be the first thing you do when you get home tonight. Take your booklets with you and share with them—that's even better."

This hit a responsive note in the young people and they nodded their approval.

It was past time for everyone to eat, but no one seemed restless, so Josh kept going. "There's one more thing we need to do. My Uncle JJ and Aunt Lynn are experienced in praying for deliverance for people who need it (and most of us do). Susie told me all about how they prayed for her and what happened. I don't quite understand it myself, so I'll be learning right along with you." Motioning toward JJ, he called him to the platform.

"You can't follow along in your booklets with this, so just set them aside. I know you don't have notebooks with you, so pay close attention and Lynn and I will make ourselves available to you after the meeting if you have questions." He was strong and kind and confident—the kind of person you could trust, the kids said later.

"This is what deliverance means: after you say the prayer of salvation, which you did tonight, Satan knows he can't own all of you, so he's willing to settle for just a little territory. This area or section is called a stronghold, which is a military term meaning 'a portion of territory that does not submit to the ruling authority.'

"Satan can't touch your spirit, because you received a new spirit when you prayed the salvation prayer. However, he has access to your soul, which is comprised of your mind (memories), your feelings (emotions) and your will. This area called your soul needs to be cleaned out so we aren't hindered in any way from our 'spirit man' growing in the Lord. Is that clear so far?"

JJ paused for a moment and the young people nodded. "Okay, that's good. Let's go on. You just received Jesus into your life and a beam of light entered you." Kids started looking around.

"No, you can't see it, but the beings in the spiritual kingdom can (angels and demons). This light is very small right now but as you pray and read your Bible and tell others what the Lord has done for you (and what He can do for them), that light gets brighter and brighter. That's enough for tonight, but who would like to know more?" What a question! Every hand went up, as he knew they would.

"Josh and I haven't had time to discuss this, but I think he'll agree. We'd like to pray for everyone to be delivered next week at the youth meeting." High fives could be seen all around the room and loud exclamations of approval. JJ had to call for order once again—these were typical teenagers celebrating a most atypical experience! With exuberance!

"There's one more thing. Lynn and I would really like to begin a regular Bible study with you here at the church. We can work out the time with Pastor Terry and Josh, but I'm going to suggest we meet at five o'clock so the basketball team can join us. We'll let all of you know in plenty of time—then you can tell your friends."

After closing in prayer, JJ and Josh agreed that it would be wise to let the youth eat and have some time of personal fellowship. They could get all the answers they needed in later sessions. What an evening! Historical, life-changing, pleasing to the Father. God be praised!

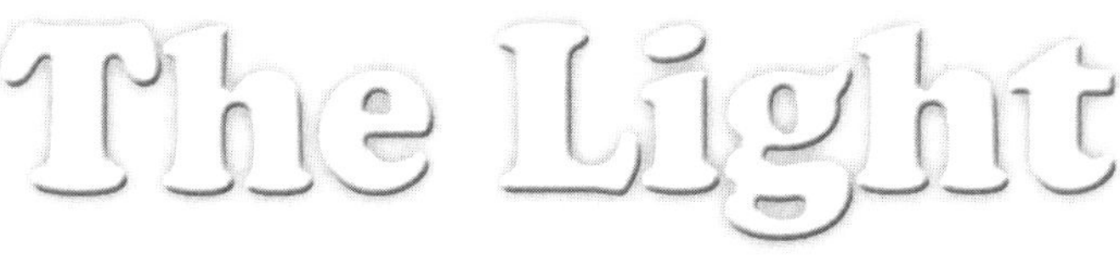

The Light

16

JJ and Lynn dismissed themselves from the youth meeting and walked down the path toward the cottage, hand in hand, hearts too full for expression. They stopped to look back toward the church through the overhanging branches and saw Josh and Susie in profile standing by the entrance. Josh leaned down and lightly kissed Susie before they turned and went back with the crowd.

"Looks like things are back to normal for those two," Lynn said, squeezing JJ's hand and smiling. "The enemy has certainly been defeated there, but what do you make of the $200,000?"

"I'm sure it's just as much of a setup as that little thing with Lisa was. We're not through here, yet, I can see that."

They were having tea and reading when the cottage vibrated from loud knocking on the door. Who on earth could that be at this time of night? Probably just one of the kids with more questions, Lynn thought, as she opened the door.

But, no! Bobbi nearly fell into the room, sobbing.

"Bobbi, what on earth is wrong with you? You look like you've been crying for hours. Come in, come in."

Bobbi was so distressed that Lynn could see she had to calm down before she could talk coherently. Lynn's heart was filled with compassion as she took Bobbi's arm and gently guided her to the sofa. Bobbi, pretty Bobbi, looked horrible, and this in itself concerned Lynn.

"Let me get you a cup of tea, Bobbi. Would you like a sandwich or some cheese?"

"No! No, thanks. I'm so sick I don't think I could eat or drink a thing."

"Well, obviously something is terribly wrong. Do you mind if JJ joins us?"

Bobbi broke into tears again and trembled, as she nodded. "Of course JJ can be here."

Gaining her composure, Bobbi continued, "I have messed things up so badly that I don't know if it can ever be fixed! This is bad, really *bad!* I can't believe what I've done."

What *had* she done? Lynn and JJ could only look at each other. "Go on, Bobbi," Lynn said softly, putting her arm around Bobbi's shoulders.

"Well, it all started with the extra offering Sunday morning—it amounted to $200,000 and every check was earmarked for the missions fund. But we don't even have a missions fund, so I didn't tell anyone about it, not even Terry, at first. I just made the deposit, as usual, then got in way over my head because of my lust."

Lust? Lynn and JJ looked at each other over her head *again*.

"What kind of lust are you talking about, Bobbi?" Lynn was very gentle.

"My lust for the old Tyndall mansion. I've wanted to live there since I was a little girl and when I found out it was for sale for only $200,000, I impulsively went to see Byron Van Cleve at the bank and put a down payment on its purchase."

Actually, JJ and Lynn were relieved to hear this description of Bobbi's "lust" but they hadn't heard the whole story.

"Then there's Pastor Bob."

This time JJ and Lynn gave each other a very pointed look. Uh oh, what was coming next?

"What about Pastor Bob?" Lynn was doing all the questioning, feeling that Bobbi would be more comfortable with that.

Trying hard not to cry, Bobbi said, "Honest, nothing happened that was so horrible, I guess, but even what happened wasn't right. Pastor Bob and I ran into each other Monday morning just before the bank opened and sat on the bench together. It was when we got into the bank that I had the idea to ask Byron Van Cleve the sale price of the mansion, because it wasn't on the sign in the front yard. Byron told me the asking price and asked if I'd like to look at the inside—but he couldn't take me himself, because he was too busy. When Pastor Bob offered to go with me, I jumped at the chance. Bad move."

"What do you mean?"

"I mean that he had started hitting on me while we were still on the bench outside the bank, so I should have had enough sense to refuse his offer. But, to be honest, I *liked* the idea! And while we at the mansion, we held hands and he kissed me, even though I knew it was wrong. Lynn, I'm ashamed to say that I was very attracted to him and didn't resist at all. I'm so embarrassed!"

"Well, was that the end of it?"

"It was for that day, but the next morning he called to tell me he was happy we were buying the house, then invited me for lunch to celebrate. I was afraid people in Centerville would talk, so we went up to the Gold Mine Restaurant. And that's where I really almost got in over my head. I don't know what came over me but I felt like I was obsessed with the man."

Now Lynn and JJ discerned what had happened! Another set-up! Part of the master plan, no doubt.

Bobbi seemed more at ease and, to be honest, she was relieved to be able to get the incident off her chest.

"We were at a window table, enjoying our lunch, when Bob reached over and took my hand. When he kissed it, I had an irresistible urge to kiss his hand, as well, and when I did, Frank Moore, the Chairman of the church Board, rushed over to our table. I didn't even know he was there. Anyway, he was nice at first, then he tore into me about being with Bob. I was so shocked that I got up and left before we finished our lunch. I felt like such a fool and it's been bothering me ever since."

"Does Terry know?"

"No, I haven't told him." Bobbi burst into tears again. "He's been so excited about this new Jesus thing in his life and about moving, that I haven't had the heart to tell him. What really surprises me is the fact that the Board hasn't told him, yet. I'm positive Frank told them all. Oh, Lynn, what am I going to do?"

Lynn and JJ remained quiet and let Bobbi sob for a few minutes. She was evidently deeply contrite and the weeping could be good for her, they felt. Lynn patted her on the back and said nothing.

"I feel like I've really messed up our family by my foolishness. I've humiliated my husband and the church family and I've just been desperate. I know this sounds so weak, but I've even been thinking of killing myself!"

Finally it was time for JJ to speak, "Bobbi, you have been the victim of an elaborate set-up by evil forces. We're certain of that! Let me ask you something. Did you eat or drink anything with Pastor Bob before the two incidents you mentioned?"

Bobbi wrinkled her brow, closed her eyes, then replied, "Let me think! On Monday morning, while we were sitting on the bench outside the bank, he held my coffee while I went to the car to retrieve my purse, but I'd bought it for myself."

"What about Tuesday?"

"On Tuesday morning, we stopped for coffee before we began the drive up to the restaurant. Why?"

JJ didn't answer Bobbi's question, instead asking another one. "Who else knows that the money was earmarked for the missions fund?"

Bobbi closed her eyes to think again, then answered, "Only Byron and the bank teller. Oh, by the way, that's who Frank was with at the Gold Mine Restaurant—Byron Van Cleve."

This "mystery" was unraveling very quickly, becoming a transparent scheme and revealing the enemy's strategy.

"Bobbi, I'm sure you can't see it, but you've been set up. In fact, your entire family has been targeted, for some reason, even Josh."

Bobbi gasped. "Josh? What's happened to Josh? Is he all right?"

"Josh is fine, Bobbi. In fact, he is wonderful—and I'm sure you'll be hearing all about it when you get home. Whatever the enemy had planned for him was completely thwarted before too much damage was done, so we give thanks to God." JJ looked at Lynn and suggested she take over.

"Bobbi," Lynn said quietly and calmly, "there is only one way to face a problem and that's head-on! I think we should call Terry and have him come over so we can all sit down together and get this sorted out. You need to be truthful and straightforward with him—I know it's scary but it's the only way."

Bobbi nodded and reached for the telephone. Somehow through her weeping she was able to get through to Terry that he needed to come to the cottage.

JJ and Lynn let Bobbi do all the talking when Terry came over and when he had heard the whole story, he folded Bobbi in his arms and comforted her. What a changed man! He was overwhelmed with compassion and his lack of anger was amazing to him. Jesus had made him new and he was able to share the love of Jesus with his wife because he was so filled with love himself. When he told Bobbi that she could experience that same love, she held onto him and sobbed, "Yes, I do want that same love in my life. I'm so sorry. Please forgive me."

Terry prayed and had Bobbi repeat after him—the same prayer he had prayed a few days earlier (he had committed it to memory). What a joyful time they all had, celebrating Bobbi's new life in Christ.

"I've been a pastor most of my life," Terry said, "and in all those years I've never known the satisfaction of leading a person to Jesus. This is marvelous! And I can tell you one thing, JJ, this is the first of many! As long as I have breath, I'll lead people to Jesus!"

As Bobbi and Terry moved toward the door to go home, he said, "Why don't you two come over in the morning? We need to strategize on how to win this war!"

Again JJ and Lynn were left speechless as they realized that God was giving almost instant maturity to this chosen family. The wisdom this father and son were exhibiting was God-sent.

Lynn turned off the light and glanced out the window. Bobbi and Terry had come over in separate cars, but she saw Terry bend down and lightly kiss Bobbi before closing her car door. Then he walked toward his car with his face turned upward toward heaven.

"Look at that, Lynn. Like father, like son!" He smiled with pride.

The Light

17

Mayor Casey pressed the "mute" button on the remote control for the television, swallowed his popcorn, and lifted the receiver.

"Mayor Casey here. Oh, hello, Lana." He wasn't thrilled to hear from her but he made sure his voice didn't betray him.

"Here? Oh, things are great, just great. Everything's right on schedule. Yes, Byron, Bob and I have been spending the days golfing. Thanks for the time off."

After listening for a moment, Mayor Casey said, "I've made sure that everything's ready for the real estate closing tomorrow morning! When do you think we should serve the papers on Pastor Terry? We want to make sure they close on the property before we make the arrest, so I suggest we wait until Monday afternoon. Then we can run JJ and Lynn out of town at the same time."

Mayor Casey always tried to leave the impression that he was doing all the work in getting details in place for whatever was coming up. A narcissistic, arrogant man, he highly overrated his abilities and importance to any given situation, and this was no exception.

"How are thing going in Washington? When will you be back? Oh, he wants you to stay there? Well, trust me, we can manage here. I know, Lana, *I know* your Leader is counting on you to get everything wrapped up in Centerville and we won't let you down! Things are okay here—so don't worry about it."

Mayor Casey held the phone away from his ear in an effort to escape Lana's screams. "Listen, you simpleton, things had *better* be okay there, because we *need* Centerville. It's the only place we haven't been hindered by that hideous *light* and we've got to continue to have a place where we can meet and receive our empowerment. We can't function without our monthly meetings, so don't blow this, Mayor. *I'm warning you!*"

Lana slammed down the phone and Mayor Casey winced, then returned to his television and popcorn. He popped the lid off another soft drink and muttered, "She said to take a few days off, so that's exactly what I'm doing. I wish she'd leave me alone."

The next morning Pastor Terry and Bobbi go up early, anticipating the closing on the property at eleven o'clock. They made their way to the cottage early as they agreed upon the night before in order to meet with JJ and Lynn for prayer and planning.

"Come in, you two," JJ greeted them. "Good to see you and glad you're so early. Terry, you need to call your Board members right away and see how fast they can get to The Lamplighter. Tell them it's an emergency and their presence is vital!"

Terry and Bobbi felt like they were on an emotional roller coaster and wondered if this was going to be an "up" or a "down" on the ride. Time would tell.

On the way over to the restaurant, JJ briefly explained that the issue of the $200,000 and the luncheon Bobbi had with Pastor Bob both needed to be discussed with the Board because they both held far-reaching implications. Not just personally, but for the church and the kingdom of God.

Almost miraculously, within half an hour they were all gathered at the restaurant. JJ instructed the waitress to bring pots of coffee, enough for everyone, then stop serving them until she was notified. He didn't want interruptions or distractions during the next hour or so.

Once again seated at the "infamous" big, round table, Pastor Terry stood before them. "Thanks again for coming on such short notice. We have two topics of discussion this morning, so let's get down to business. I know you all know about the $200,000 the church received in the office a week ago—has it been only a week?—and there's another subject we need to discuss, too, which has to do with Bobbi and Pastor Bob. Uncle JJ has a lot of knowledge and wisdom about the enemy and his tactics and I want him to explain to you what's going on." Pastor Terry looked somber, then his face brightened for a moment.

"Oh, by the way, Bobbi said the prayer last night, too, and now she's one of us!" There were excited, but subdued, exclamations of joy at the good news. They looked over where Bobbi and Lynn were sitting close together and smiled.

JJ began his explanation of how Bobbi, Josh, Terri, and the church had been set up.

"Initially, the plan of Satan was to eliminate Lynn and me because we were coming to Centerville filled with *the light*. But when that plan failed, and Pastor Terry became born again, they enlarged the strategy to include his entire family and the church. Mayor Casey, Pastor Bob and Byron Van Cleve are cooperating with the evildoers to get Pastor Terry out of the picture. They have seen *the light* shining in him, but they have no idea that this morning the light is shining on almost every street in Centerville. You should have been at the youth meeting last night!"

Frank Moore spoke up, "What about the closing, JJ? Is it illegal to buy the mansion with church money? We have consulted with tax experts and others, trying to keep the purchase aboveboard, but I'm still concerned that we might get in trouble. What do you think?"

"Well, let's look at it here for a minute. I know some steps have been taken that might jeopardize the church, and we can be sure that the devil means to turn things so that the church will be damaged. But God can take what the devil meant for bad and turn it into good!"

The faces around the table took on hopeful looks and JJ had their full attention. "Also, the Word of God says in Proverbs 13:22 that the wealth of the wicked is laid up for the righteous. So why don't we put our heads together and see if we can beat them at their own game!"

Pausing to look at his watch, JJ said to Terry and Bobbi, "It's later than I thought, so why don't you two meet with the other parties and get ready to take care of the closing on the mansion. We'll stay here and see what kind of strategy we can put into place. But first, let's join hands and pray together."

The Light

18

The property closing went without a hitch and by Saturday afternoon almost the entire congregation of Centerville Christian Center had gathered to help Pastor Terry, Bobbi and Josh move the few belongings they had kept to take to the mansion—their new home! It didn't take long, and since the women of the church had cooked what looked like a feast for the occasion, they set up tables outside and had a big party at the *new* mansion.

Such excitement. Teenagers crowded the pool, the tennis courts and basketball courts. After everyone was fed, the ladies occupied themselves by strolling from room to room admiring the furnishings and décor. The older guys went to the lake with their fishing equipment and took some of the boats out on the water. It had turned out to be a thoroughly enjoyable day, after all.

Just at sundown, Pastor Terry had everyone come together for a prayer of thanksgiving and blessing upon the house. Their hearts were too full for adequate expression, but the pastor and his wife tried to convey their love and appreciation.

After everyone left, Pastor Terry, Bobbi and Josh went inside, held hands and said their own family prayer of thanksgiving for God's unbelievable gift to them—not the mansion, but salvation! The mansion was the "icing on the cake."

Pastor Terry and Bobbi retired to the master suite and found their bed turned down and fresh flowers on the dresser. Propped against the vase was a note:

We love our pastor and his family

Knocking on Josh's bedroom door, Pastor Terry said softly, "Josh, I think you'd like to see this." Josh was equally overwhelmed at the love and warmth conveyed in the note.

Tears of joy streamed down Bobbi's face as she remembered playing in this very bedroom as a girl. "I can hardly believe that I told my friends that someday this would be my bedroom. It's hard to fathom—but here I am! Thank you, Lord."

Josh quietly exited and left his parents alone. Bobbi was still praising the Lord for His goodness when she turned to her husband, "Terry, I think God just gave the devil enough rope to hang himself."

Terry just smiled, took his wife's hand, and whispered, "We've got a full day tomorrow. I have a feeling the service is going to be phenomenal—and different!"

He was right, of course. Sunday morning's service was a blowout! Centerville had never experienced a church service like that before but it was the fulfillment of Terry's grandfather's dream—and what he had prayed for his entire life. The people sang God's praises with exuberance and worshipped with sincerely grateful hearts.

Many in the congregation raised their hands to get permission to share what God had done for them. Pastor Terry was happy to allow a few testimonies, but he had to cut it off in order to get on with the service. After all, they had a special speaker this morning.

"You are all so welcome here this morning and you can see that many miracles have been performed since we last gathered here. I'm going to have my uncle come forward in just a moment to share from God's Word but first, I have an announcement. Let's do something different! To my knowledge, this church has never had a Sunday night service and I think we should start a trend tonight. Let's meet at six o'clock here in the sanctuary and share some more about God's goodness to all of us! What do you say?"

As he anticipated, the place broke into spontaneous applause—the youth (most of whom had brought their parents) were especially noisy and enthusiastic. "Okay, that settles it. We will inaugurate our new Sunday evening service tonight! Now, let's pay close attention as JJ ministers the Word of God to us."

What a difference in the atmosphere! Those present were attentive and supportive and when JJ asked if anyone would like to receive Jesus as Savior, people ran down the aisle toward the altar before he finished asking. Although there were no trained counselors in the church (they had never needed any), Board members and young people gathered around the new converts and began praying and reading the Word to them. What a miracle!

As JJ and Lynn left the church together, she said to him, "Honey, I think you were right! We were on a mission and I'm so thankful we didn't let Satan deter us with his tricks. And I'm glad you didn't listen to my foolish suggestion that we turn around and leave town." They smiled at each other with understanding.

There were enough delectable leftovers from Saturday's party to provide a lovely after-church lunch, so JJ and Lynn joined Terry, Bobbi and Josh on the porch overlooking the beautiful lake. Oh, and Susie was there, which made it seem perfect. Josh had not heard from Lisa and, to everyone's deep relief, her name was never again mentioned.

"Terry and I want you to move all your stuff over here to one of the guest rooms and stay with us as long as you can. There's so much more room here and we'd love to have you." Bobbi was so happy in her new home that she wanted to share it with those she loved.

"Bobbi, you're so thoughtful, and we're grateful, but we're really on a roll with the book and it wouldn't be good to interrupt the process now." JJ tried to explain further, "The anointing of the Holy Spirit is flowing and the book is coming together better than we could have dreamed, so we need to stay put and get it finished."

Turning toward Terry, JJ said, "You know, Terry, I was overseas serving as a missionary when your dad moved to Centerville and we almost lost touch with each other for many years. I was still in Africa when your grandpa died and barely got home in time for his funeral. Then when your mom and dad died in the accident, word didn't reach me in time to get home because I was ministering in the bush country. News doesn't travel very fast out there, you know. I knew that the church had built a little cottage for Dad to live in and he wrote me about how pleased he was."

"Yeah, that seemed to make him happy. I loved going to the cottage to spend time with him." Terry smiled at the memory.

"Do you remember me ever mentioning Dad burying my mother's Bible under the cottage?"

Puzzled, Terry answered, "No, never. In fact, I'm not sure what you're talking about, JJ."

"Well, I'd forgotten about it until we started working on the book in the cottage, but Dad wrote and said he had put Mom's Bible in plastic, then placed it in a metal box and buried it in the ground. Of course, this was before they poured the cement for the foundation. Somehow I feel that there's a connection between Mom's Bible and the anointing that has been on our work. We worked on this book for years and couldn't seem to get anywhere, but as soon as we settled into the cottage, it just opened up."

"That's absolutely amazing, JJ, but for some reason I believe you're right!"

"I hadn't thought about that for years but Lynn and I were talking about the special anointing and she reminded me of the letter from Dad and the Bible under the foundation. We felt that we should stay in Centerville for a little longer than we had planned and pour our knowledge into the new Christians. They are hungry to learn God's Word and we would be thrilled to stay and teach them."

"JJ, you have no idea what a relief that is. I had asked the Lord for some sort of provision to teach the people, because I have so much to learn myself. Why didn't I think of asking you? So much has been going on that I'm not thinking straight. We'll set up some special study groups immediately. How long do you think you can stay with us?"

"I would imagine a few weeks. It looks like the book will be finished this week, then we can devote ourselves to study in preparation for the sessions at church. We'll also probably be getting into a lot of deliverance. I would prefer not to start that until the book is completely done because it can be exhausting."

They realized they have been relaxing and talking for hours and they needed to prepare for the evening service. And preparation included *rest* for the adults. Josh and Susie had been out on the lake boating for quite a while.

The historic Sunday evening service exceeded the expectations of the pastor and his wife. The auditorium was full before starting time and excitement filled the air! Pastor Terry was glad he had decided to start the service at six o'clock because the congregation seemed to want to continue singing praise and worship songs over and over. Shouts of joy could be heard down the street from the church and the new

Christians marveled at the difference in the people and the church. *The light* glowed so brightly that it could be seen for blocks—if there had been anyone around to observe it.

The Light

19

Lana roused herself from her nap as she heard the private plane make its usual shifts in sound in preparation for landing. The sky outside seemed unusually bright for the evening hour but she assumed the moon was exceptionally bright and thought no more of it. As the plane banked on its final approach, however, Lana glanced out the window and let out a bloodcurdling scream. Even though the pilot saw it, too, his primary job was to land the plane safely before this crazy woman opened the door and jumped out! He was accustomed to her occasional tantrums but today's incessant screeching was unnerving.

The instant the plane came to a halt, the pilot jumped from his seat, unlatched the door and let the "crazy woman" exit. He was afraid she'd break the door down if she got to it before he did. Even though only one limousine met the plane, The Big Three all came out to greet her, wearing huge victory grins. The instant they saw (and *heard*) her, however, their expressions changed and they were gripped with terror.

"You jerks! You idiots! What is there to smile about? Are you completely insane? Are you *blind*?" As she approached them, she started flailing her arms, and as soon as she could reach them, she hit them with surprising force.

"What are you doing, Lana? Stop it!" Her punches were doing some damage and the men had to go on the defensive.

Lana was in no mood to be reasoned with and she continued striking out as they forced her into the limo.

"You stupid dolts! *The light* is so bright in this town that I could see it from the plane. It looks like the Fourth of July over on the south end of Main Street. What have you morons been doing all weekend? You should know what's going on around here!"

There seemed to be no end to her abuse as she kicked and screamed and thrashed out at them. They were able to restrain her but for such a tiny woman, she "packed a mighty wallop," as one of the men noted.

As the driver pulled onto Main Street and slowly made his way south, the three men saw the light, as well. It looked like hundreds of beams of light radiating from one place. Could it be? As they came closer, they knew there was no mistaking the origin of the lights—Centerville Christian Center, Pastor Terry's church!

Lana's hands flew to her face and covered her eyes. "I can't stand the light! Get me out of here—it's blinding me!" Then, turning to The Big Three, she shrieked, "*How could this happen*? I told you to watch things around here. I'll bet you've done nothing but golf the whole time I've been gone!" Which was pretty close to the truth.

Instructing the driver to get them to Mayor Casey's mansion quickly, Lana picked up her cell phone and called Darlene and Lisa. "GET OVER TO THE MAYOR'S MANSION RIGHT AWAY!" That's all she said, but she knew her command would be obeyed.

Arriving at the mansion, the four piled out of the limo and started toward the front door. Lana seemed to have calmed down, although she was still pushing the men around. Lana shoved the men through the door and in an instant she turned into a monster—a beast! She blew up into a hideous creature with fire coming from its nose. The repulsive, vile "thing" hissed and snarled, causing the men to recoil in horror, and even though they had seen this happen to a lesser degree in the past, they were unprepared for what happened next. The ugly creature *developed long claws* and stormed around the room slashing furniture, ripping off wallpaper and breaking valuable crystal. The Big Three feared they might be next.

Darlene and Lisa arrived, mystified by all the noise. As Lisa looked at her mom for an explanation, realization dawned on Darlene and terror showed on her face. Lisa didn't know enough to be scared, because she had not yet seen Lana's metamorphosis.

Darlene, however, had seen Lana morph into the beast once before and she had an idea of what was in store for all of them.

Entering the room where the beast was tearing things up, Lisa understood why her mom was scared. Probably because of her youth and relative inexperience, Lisa was curious and wanted to go closer, but her mother screamed out a warning, "No, Lisa! Don't go near it! Those claws could rip you to shreds in a second. This is no time to be naïve. This is one beast you can't tame—I've even seen it eat people before."

The Big Three cowered in the corner and when they overheard what Darlene said, they put their arms around each other like little boys. Lisa thought she heard Mayor Casey whimpering—or was it her imagination?

Darlene held Lisa and all five stayed as far away from the beast as they could, relieved when it continued its rampage in other parts of the house. They could hear it stomp from room to room and after about eight or ten minutes, Lana transmuted back into her original form and returned. No one in the room ever imagined they would be glad to see Lana in her usual state! They were just glad "it" hadn't felt inclined to harm—or eat!—any of them.

But Lana was still incensed, although the target of her anger shifted. Now she raged about JJ and Lynn, "I hate those two! Hate! Hate! Hate! And our Leader hates them, too! In fact, in all the universe, his number-one goal is to eliminate them, because of the book they're writing."

"What book?" Lisa whispered to her mother.

"Shhhhhhh!" Darlene made no sound but Lisa understood.

"That book, little Lisa, could be a major defeat for us. If it gets published, Christians all over the world will be made aware of our tactics and they'll know how to overcome us. Right now Christians are so ignorant that they don't pay any attention to us; in fact, many of them don't even believe we exist—and that's the way we like it. The greatest weapon in our arsenal is convincing them to ignore us and so far we've kept them fooled. We've deceived them into believing that deliverance isn't for today and that it isn't even of God, so they stay away from it out of fear. But somehow the light got into Pastor Terry and he not only wants to take Centerville, but he's planning on taking the whole world for Jesus!"

"But, Lana..."

"Shut up, Lisa! I don't have time to discuss this with you." Lana began to wring her hands and wail, "What am I going to do?"

"GET OUT OF HERE, ALL OF YOU! I've got to think and you have work to do, too. Byron, call the Board members of Terry's church and arrange a meeting for tomorrow morning at eight o'clock in their conference room. I don't want it to be held in a public place. Mayor, you need to show up at the Board meeting with your arrest warrant in hand. And Pastor Bob, you go down with Mayor Casey and tell everyone within earshot about you and Bobbi Murphy."

Lisa clung to Darlene, hoping that they could just quietly leave, but it wasn't to be.

"We'll all meet tomorrow at noon at The Lamplighter and I want to hear nothing but positive reports. Lisa! You've obviously let up on paying attention to Josh and you've got to be sure you're still in control there. When you see him at school tomorrow, make him come with you to eat at The Lamplighter instead of in the school cafeteria, because we may need him. Do whatever you need to get him there. I may not be able to get rid of the light at this late date, but I can be sure we get revenge on that family and those two meddling fools over in the cottage!"

Everyone scrambled for the door with Lana's loud voice echoing in their ears, "Now get out of here and start taking care of business. I'm ashamed of all of you! You're an embarrassment! Do I have to do everything myself? I've been out fighting the light and you've all been asleep at the wheel!"

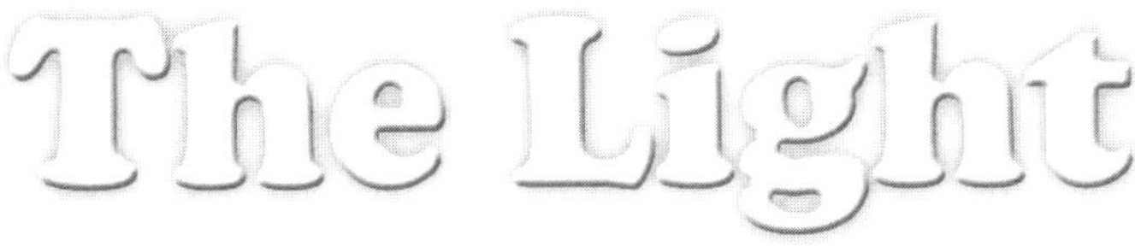

The Light

20

Josh drove by Susie's house to pick her up for school, like he often did. Their relationship was back on track and because they now had Jesus in their lives, it was better than ever. Before he pulled out of Susie's driveway, the two bowed their heads, joined hands, and prayed together, just like JJ had taught them. They both knew they needed wisdom and discernment, and thankfully, they knew the Source of all they needed!

The two stood around talking until the bell rang, then parted ways at the Media Center, going to their individual classes. Josh was content—thankful his relationship with Susie was strong again—and didn't even notice Lisa slither in, wearing a skirt so short that it barely qualified as a skirt.

As usual, Lisa's attire, grooming and body language screamed for attention—and she was getting plenty! However, Josh seemed oblivious to her presence until she inched her chair close to his and whispered provocatively, "Joshie, I've really missed you!"

Josh instinctively pulled away and felt an unexpected revulsion overtake him as he took her hand off his arm. She seemed not to notice, however, and kept right on talking. "I've got the greatest idea! Instead of eating lunch here, why don't we run over to The Lamplighter? We'll have plenty of time. My mom's going to be there with some friends and I want you to meet her."

Finally she noticed the change in Josh and fear gripped her. What was going on?

Josh looked at Lisa as she moved her chair back to its original position and realized that he now saw her with "new eyes" since he had accepted Jesus into his life. Instead of vibrant beauty, he saw emptiness and desperation. "Thank you, Lord, for bringing me into Your truth," he whispered under his breath.

"No, Lisa, that's *not* a great idea. I'm having lunch with Susie today and you might as well know that I'll be having lunch with her every day from now on. We've been together for a long time and we believe we have a future together. I'm sorry about what happened between you and me the other day."

Lisa's voice was urgent, *"What are you talking about?"* Then she glanced at Josh's neck and almost went into shock. "Where's the necklace, Josh? Where's the necklace I gave you? You promised me you wouldn't take it off, but you have, haven't you?"

Josh pulled the necklace from his pocked and handed it to her, giving in to the impulse to needle her just a little. "You need to get that thing recharged—it's lost all its power."

Lisa lost control! Without saying a word, she stood up, stomped her feet and glared at Josh. The expression on her face turned from seductive to hideous, and she stormed out of the room, huffing and puffing like a bull in the ring ready to fight.

Mr. Russell was on his feet like a flash and grabbed her arm just as she started down the hall.

"Come back here, young lady! You may get away with that in some schools, but I don't allow that kind of behavior in my class. If you're so determined to go someplace, get yourself down to the principal's office. I'll be there right behind you." He let go of her arm and tried to return to his classroom, but Lisa wouldn't let go of him. In fact, she began to beat him around the face and neck, then threw him to the floor, and he was shocked at her strength. Heavens! This girl had the strength of two grown men. He made a defensive move and let out a mild oath as the students sat in stunned silence, spellbound.

Mr. Russell couldn't know that Lisa was, indeed, desperate. She knew she was in trouble with Lana and if she failed with Josh, their Leader would find out about it and she could lose everything, maybe even her life. She was out of control but she couldn't help herself. She acted like a wild animal and the teacher felt like he was in real danger, so he stayed on the floor.

Josh jumped out of his seat! "I command you to stop, in the Name of Jesus!" The voice of authority came out of this young man, another shock for his classmates, although they knew he had courage.

Lisa immediately went limp and almost fell, then with a glance that contained intense malice, she ran from the building. She let Josh know in that one look that she intended to retaliate.

Mr. Russell allowed Josh to help him up from the floor and asked, "What's going on, Josh? What was that all about?"

"Just some light driving out some darkness," Josh replied cryptically.

"I'm sure you know I have no idea what you're talking about," Mr. Russell said, looking at his young student. He rubbed his face lightly and carefully. "That was a fierce attack by such a small girl."

Many of Josh's classmates had accepted Jesus and were watching expectantly to see what Josh would say.

"As strange as it may seem, Mr. Russell, there is an explanation for what just happened. Lisa was sent to this school by a wicked leader, the devil, to do evil—but the plan just backfired. When I accepted Jesus into my life, I became a different person and now I'm able to discern light from darkness—and Lisa walks in darkness."

Some of the guys groaned when they heard Josh say that Lisa was evil. Not that gorgeous creature! Surely she couldn't be bad.

Mr. Russell just looked at Josh, waiting for him to continue. However, Josh took at pamphlet out of his pocked and handed it to the teacher. "Here, Mr. Russell, I'd like to give you this little booklet to read and I'd be glad to discuss it with you later if you want to."

Still saying nothing, Mr. Russell accepted the booklet and stuffed it into his briefcase.

"Oh, one more thing, Mr. Russell. Could I be excused for a few minutes to go talk to Coach Doug? I want to see if he'll reinstate me to the basketball team. What I did was really stupid—maybe he'll have pity on me." He grinned as Mr. Russell told him to *go*.

As one, the students stood and broke into spontaneous applause—with Mr. Russell joining in!

The Light

21

The Board members had all been notified of the meeting at the church, and Frank had called Pastor Terry and Bobbi to make sure they attended, along with JJ and Lynn. Why JJ and Lynn? Just a feeling he had. He *thought* it was a hunch but he would soon learn to discern the voice of the Lord.

The Big Three arrived in a police car, an indulgence afforded Mayor Casey, and they could hardly contain their glee. They entered the room like Olympic gold medal winners, with shoulders squared and eyes glowing, trying not to gloat. Their spirits sagged a bit when they saw the four unexpected visitors. What were *they* doing at the secret Board meeting? Mayor Casey had specifically specified "Board members only" and he wasn't pleased with what he considered a violation of his instructions, although he could have anticipated Pastor Terry's presence.

Frank Moore, as Chairman, greeted everyone and called the meeting to order. Out of the corner of his eye, he could see the police car still parked outside the church.

Mayor Casey, not wanting to submit to anyone else's "order," interrupted, "I wasn't expecting non-Board members to be here, but I guess it's just as well that Pastor Terry and his wife are present, because we have some business to conduct with them." Surprisingly, the Mayor seemed to be ignorant of basic church ethics. The church Board members never met without their pastor present, under any circumstances.

Frank was tolerant, "What kind of business, Mayor?"

"The Chief of Police gave us a ride over and is waiting outside with another police officer, because Pastor Terry is to be arrested this morning." He failed to mention that he planned to have the Board members arrested, as well.

This statement was too ludicrous to be taken seriously, but Frank managed to ask, "On what charge, Mayor?"

"Fraud!" the Mayor snapped.

None of the Board members seemed shaken, because they knew the business of the church and they felt they knew their pastor intimately. He had never given them cause to question his integrity, either personally or in his business dealings.

"I'm afraid you're going to have to explain yourself, Mayor Casey, because none of us is about to let anyone arrest our pastor." Frank's voice rang with confidence and purpose.

Mayor Casey came back just as confidently, "We'll see about that, Frank. Byron here is president of the bank, as you know, and he can prove that the Tyndall mansion was purchased with misappropriated church funds. The money was donated with the express purpose of being used for missions—and it wasn't! That's FRAUD, pure and simple! We can document everything. Do you have anything to say before we handcuff Pastor Terry and take him in?"

Pastor Terry, Bobbi, JJ and Lynn listened to the two men in disbelief—yet, somehow, knowing that it was another part of the set-up. Disbelief turned to dismay as the men continued, then became simply interesting as a peace settled on the four of them because they knew the enemy! And they knew ultimate victory was on its way. "Wonder how the Lord is going to work all this out" was the prevailing thought in their minds. Watch and learn.

Frank Moore was on his feet and several others looked like they were more than ready to speak, as well.

"You bet I have something to say, and by the looks of things, I'm not the only one!" Frank knew anger was not in order, so he kept his emotions in check. "That mansion is church property, you're right about that, but it's not wholly for the pastor and his family. We discussed the missions aspect at length and came to several conclusions regarding missionaries. But, Mayor Casey, we are under no obligation to discuss these private church matters with you. Go ahead and have the Chief come in and arrest Pastor Terry—then see what happens when you have to answer for instigating a false arrest."

Mayor Casey looked at Byron and Pastor Bob and his face almost crumpled when he thought of the noon meeting with Lana. What if they failed here? He lost some of his bluster and approached Frank in a conciliatory manner.

"You're right, Frank, you don't have to divulge any private matters to us, but could you give us a little more information?" He knew they had to be loaded with persuasive facts before they met Lana. Frank almost pitied him.

"Well, Mayor, even though Pastor Terry and his family will be the primary residents of the mansion, it's so large that it can be used for many other purposes. For instance, the entire third floor has been designated as a place for visiting missionaries to rest and be refreshed. Beyond that, a full-scale retreat is being planned for next year, so that many more missionaries can enjoy the facilities at one time. Pastor Terry's Uncle JJ served overseas in missions for many years and he has agreed to supervise this outreach. He's going to start with dozens of missionaries from around the world that he knows personally. So, you see, we've done a lot of planning and thinking this past week—and *fraud* was not involved!"

The Big Three looked at each other in terror, trying to remain calm, as Mayor Casey spoke again, "Sounds like you've been doing your homework, all right."

"Yes, we have, and we were up early this morning doing more. We voted to change the name of the place from Tyndall Mansion to The International Missionary Resort! Now, Mayor Casey, what could be illegal about that?"

Mayor Casey's chubby features appeared downright crestfallen and he was tempted to admit defeat when Pastor Bob stood up. He thought maybe he could save the day, since it looked the fraud deal wasn't going to go over.

"Pastor Terry and members of the Board, I have a confession to make which affects you all. Bobbi Murphy and I have been seeing each other and we've become quite intimate!"

Holding hands,Terry and Bobbi had wondered how long it would take Pastor Bob to drop his "bombshell" on the group.

Pastor Terry dropped Bobbi's hand, looked Pastor Bob directly in the eye and spoke firmly, "Bob, it's a well-known fact in Centerville that you have tried to seduce many unsuspecting women around these parts and no one has ever stopped you. You've gotten away with it because nobody really cared. But, my friend, things have changed in Centerville since Uncle JJ and Lynn brought *the light* to this town of utter darkness. Your days of charm, women and *coffee* are over!"

Pastor Bob slumped down in his chair and groaned in disbelief. Had he heard correctly? *Coffee?* How could Pastor Terry know about that? How could *anyone* know about the coffee and the potion?

Memories of Lana spewing out her threats assaulted Pastor Bob's mind. "If you ever cross our Leader, you'll find yourself lying in a heap somewhere." Could she have meant *literally* lying in a heap? Maybe so, because she had also told Lisa that if she messed up, she would lose her looks and sex appeal.

"Oh, man, I've messed up *big time*." Putting his head in his hands, he slumped deeper into his chair. What could he say now? They were on to him if they knew about the coffee.

While Pastor Bob was wallowing in misery and self-pity, Mayor Casey and Byron Van Cleve huddled in a corner, whispering. "Byron, that beast Lana morphed into last night scared me half to death, how about you?"

"I'm still shaken by it, Mayor, I don't mind admitting. In fact, it's all I've been able to think about all night—I've never even heard of such a thing in my life. Darlene said she'd seen the beast eat people—do you think that could be true? I can't believe it, but then, knowing Lana, I guess it's possible. What're we going to do? If she gets hold of us after today, it's all over. I don't think she'd eat us, *but who knows?*"

Back in the center of the room, JJ reached down to Pastor Bob sitting in the chair and placed his arm across his shoulders. "Pastor Bob, you've been tormented by this spirit of seduction for a long time, haven't you? I know Lana calls it 'charm' but it's really an evil spirit that entered you sometime in the past."

Pastor Bob's whole body shook as he began to sob. "Can you tell me when all this began, Pastor Bob?" JJ gently asked.

Stifling his sobs, Pastor Bob shared, "When I was ten years old, my dad took me to a secret monthly meeting which I later learned had to do with the occult. Lana was there and she was in charge, as she *always* is," Pastor Bob said bitterly.

"All the other twelve were there, too. Come to think of it, after all these years not one of them has changed—they don't age! Isn't that odd?" Not so odd when you know the facts.

"Well, anyway, Lana made me the center of attention that night and the first thing they had me do was drink some fruit juice. It tasted bitter and I told my dad I didn't like it, but he made me drink every drop. My head turned to stone and I don't remember anything that happened the rest of the night."

"How long were you unconscious?"

"I'm not sure of the length of time, but when I woke up, the sun was coming up and I was lying on top of the old well out at the abandoned Furman Ranch. Only my dad was there with me and he told me the weirdest stuff. He said I'd never have to worry about anything my whole life, that I would have money and charisma and appeal and excellent health. Neither of us ever mentioned it again."

JJ spoke up, "Pastor Bob, you don't realize it, perhaps, but you have been in bondage to Lana all these years. Would you like to be free?"

Pastor Bob blurted, "Right now, I'd give everything I own not to have to face her again. But how can I be free of her? She'd kill me before she'd let me go."

"It seems that way, I know, but there's a curse on your life and you can be set free. I can break that curse right now through the power of Jesus Christ."

Wow! This Board meeting had certainly taken a curious turn. No one was making a sound and all eyes were on JJ.

"JJ, I'm trying to understand, but this is all new to me. Is that the power that comes into humans and causes the light to shine in them? I can see *the light,* you know. I can see it in all of you and I saw it in your father, but I haven't seen it in anyone for fifteen years until you two came to town."

JJ was happy to explain, "You're right. When a person accepts Jesus as their Lord and Savior, the light enters them and at that moment they have all power over the entire demonic kingdom. The great news for you is that you can have the light in you and you won't be in bondage to Lana anymore. Pastor Bob, do you want the light? Do you believe what I'm telling you?"

Pastor Bob wanted to make a wise choice, so he didn't answer right away. After thinking a moment, he replied, "It must be true. I see it in all of you and now that you've explained that the person with Jesus has power over the demonic realm, I figure that must be why Lana's so afraid of it. Her sole mission in life is to get rid of the light. I know she's terrified of you, JJ, and Lynn. And she's also scared of the book you're writing, because she says it will inform and enlighten Christians, leading to her defeat. That must be *some book!* And in answer to your question, YES, I WANT IT!"

Pastor Terry had won many souls to the Lord over the past few days and he jumped up with a shout, "Pastor Bob, let me do the honors. Repeat this prayer after me!"

What a sight—the two local pastors embracing each other and bowing before the Lord. It was beautiful, and everyone in the room was deeply moved. When they finished praying, Pastor Bob glanced down at his chest and exclaimed, "I see it! A beam of light just entered me. And the singing! Can you hear the singing? It sounds like a million-voice choir. WOW!"

Mayor Casey and Byron were the only others in the room who saw the beam of light enter him, and they were astonished. What was going to happen to The Big Three now—would it become The Big Two? They knew Pastor Bob was no longer one of them!

"Pastor Bob, there's one more step you need to take so that you will have no fear of Lana or her Leader."

"But I have no fear now, JJ! What could be better than this? But I'll do anything you say."

"I want to pray with you, Pastor Bob, so that you can be free and stay free forever."

JJ prayed, *"Father, right now, in the Name of Jesus, I break every ungodly (emotional) soul tie between Pastor Bob and Lana and the other twelve members of her group. I put a Jesus bloodline between them and, Satan, you and your kingdom will never again cross that bloodline!"*

"Now, Pastor Bob, I want you to repeat after me." Pastor Bob indicated he would.

"I renounce anything that I have ever done in the occult. I am sorry and I ask You, heavenly Father, to forgive me and wash me clean with the blood of Jesus."

Pastor Bob repeated the prayer, then JJ prayed loudly, *"Now, in the Name of Jesus, I command any demonic forces that entered Pastor Bob through his occult activities to leave him now!"*

Pastor Bob sat up straight, lifted his head high, and screamed at the top of his lungs. Then it was OVER! He slumped back down into his chair, looked around the room and started laughing. His joy was so evident that everyone else rejoiced with him.

Everyone except Mayor Casey and Byron Van Cleve. They were agitated, uneasy, frightened. Had Bob lost his mind?

"What's wrong with you?" Mayor Casey blurted out, running over to Pastor Bob and grabbing him by the shoulder.

Pastor Bob jumped from his chair and grabbed both his friends in a bear hug. "I don't know what you call it, boys," he said between laughs, "but you'd better get some of this. I've never felt this much joy in my whole life!"

Pastor Terry couldn't let such a golden opportunity pass him by—he saw two prospective souls to be won and he wanted to be the ones to lead them to the Savior.

"Are you two ready? You can have this joy and freedom, too!"

"Not so fast!" Byron was reserved by nature and this looked a little too emotional and theatrical for his taste. But Mayor Casey looked ready! And when Byron looked at Pastor Bob, then at his other friend, Mayor

Casey, he felt he had the answer: Yes, God is real—and I really *do* want what Pastor Bob has!

The "Big Two" told Pastor Terry they were ready to pray with him and more tears were shed. What a blessed time! At the end of the prayer, Mayor Casey and Byron looked at each other and saw the beam of light enter into them. They fell to their knees in wonder and as the tears turned to laughter, they joined with all the others singing, dancing and praising God. It was glorious!

The police officers were still parked outside, undoubtedly wondering what on earth was taking place inside. They had expected to be finished with their business long before now.

Bobbi went over to the old piano in the corner of the conference room and started playing worship songs on the out-of-tune relic. It didn't matter to the worshippers—they were busy having a victory celebration!

After over an hour of rejoicing and almost raising the roof, Mayor Casey looked at his watch. "Oh, no! Look at the time. It's almost time to go meet the beast!"

The Big Three were the only ones who actually knew what he meant, and they laughed as they gathered up their coats and prepared to leave for the restaurant. They should have been nervous but they were so filled with joy that they felt giddy and carefree. They asked everyone to have a short, specific prayer for them, then they went out to the waiting patrol car and departed, and with sirens screaming, they made their way through town.

Sitting in the restaurant with Darlene and Lisa, Lana was silent, her black eyes stone cold. She hated waiting and although the three weren't late, it was going to be close.

Within minutes the tiny bell over the door made its familiar sound and Lana involuntarily looked to see who has entering. What she saw astounded her and she reacted like a wild woman, pounding the table and screaming, "Lisa, you botched your assignment with Josh and now those pig-headed idiots obviously have botched theirs! They look like the three stooges—look at them! They look like they're drunk. AND THEY HAVE THE LIGHT IN THEM!"

Grabbing her purse, Lana bolted for the back door, preferring to exit through the kitchen. The cooks and wait staff didn't know whether to be amused or scared as they heard her scream at the two women with her, "Come on, let's get out of here *right now*!"

Lana reached for her cell phone to notify her pilot to get the plane ready, still screaming at Darlene and Lisa, "Do you realize I used our Leader's money to fund the mansion for those people? Oh, this means big trouble. Oh, oh, oh!" She sounded dismayed and disgusted at the same time.

Somehow they got to the airstrip and on their way out of Centerville. Darlene and Lisa said nothing, and Lana never stopped fuming and snarling. On the plane, Lana looked at Lisa, "The only thing that saved you, young lady, is that we need you now more than ever! There's lots of corruption in Washington, D.C. and lust runs rampant, so you will be very useful to us. Don't fail this time, though! When I was with our Leader there, he told me that he has set up some major strongholds and we should have a pretty easy job, because there isn't much light."

Back in Centerville, JJ and Lynn stayed in the cottage and continued their ministry, holding Bible studies and deliverance sessions for all who wished to attend. Revival broke out in both churches on Main Street and they conducted almost nightly meetings because the people were hungry for more of God's presence.

The relationship between JJ and Lynn and Terry and his family had deepened and they spent many happy hours together at the mansion. However, after several weeks, JJ and Lynn knew it was time to move on. The book was completed and, in fact, they felt their mission was also completed. It was hard to leave.

"JJ, remember how clean Centerville looked on the outside when we drove into town—but we both knew there was evil under the surface? Well, now Centerville is clean on the inside as well as on the outside! What a major difference!" They drove away full of joy and gratitude to God for what He had done.

They drove leisurely, enjoying each other's company and viewing the wonders of God before pulling into their own familiar driveway several days later.

JJ squinted at two men sitting on the top step of their front porch, holding their dog. "Lynn, wake up! Aren't those the two men that saved us when we almost fell over the cliff?"

"Sure looks like them. And there's Dudley!" Dudley leaped out of the arms of the man holding him and bounded toward JJ and Lynn, almost knocking them over. He was barking and licking their faces furiously (and sloppily).

After giving Dudley fond attention, they turned toward the men on the porch.

"Welcome home, friends! There's a little present for you up by the door."

JJ and Lynn saw the box lying on the porch and turned back to the men with questioning looks.

Both men smiled widely and one explained, "When we found Dudley, he had a girlfriend, a stray with no owner, and they are now the proud parents of four puppies!"

Tearing into the box, Lynn saw four absolutely adorable, cuddly puppies. Her "oohs and ahs" convinced JJ to take a peek, so he leaned over to view his new "grandkids," then turned around to talk some more to the two men.

"Lynn! They're gone!" Sure enough, the men had vanished again.

Lynn popped her head up from the puppies and saw that he was right. "Just like before," she murmured. "And we still didn't get a chance to say thank you—just like before."

"By the way, Honey, while you were napping in the car, the Lord spoke to my heart and reminded me of an old buddy who's a publisher in the Washington, D.C. area. After a few days of rest, I think we should see if Matt and Cindy can stay in our house and watch Dudley and his new family while we go to Washington. Let's take off as soon as possible!"

Claire, and her husband Paul, minister nationally and have seen thousands of people freed from demonic influence. They each hold a degree of Ph.D. in Clinical Christian Psychology, and conduct private and group counseling sessions. They also conduct seminars and teach a School of Deliverance.

Other books from Warefare Plus Ministries

THIS MEANS WAR! - A complete guide to the teachings of Christ on deliverance, along with many other biblical references regarding deliverance. Sadly, deliverance has been treated almost like a forbidden topic in the church realm. THIS MEANS WAR! teaches in great depth everything you always wanted to know about demon warfare and the supernatural, but have been afraid to ask!

DEMON SLAYERS - Actual case histories of people who have gone through deliverance. Relive the experiences with them as this book takes you through shocking, extreme, intense battles of Good versus Evil—and Good always prevails!

DELAYED INVASION - A U.S. military crew in Germany mysteriously intercepts a plot by demon entities to overthrow the governments of the world by disguising themselves as beings from outer space. Go with JJ and Lynn as they visit Washington, D.C. and get caught up in the middle of the invasion plans.

DECEIVED - Worldwide revival is taking place on planet Earth and people everywhere are uniting, with Christ as the common denominator. Satan and Lana have devised a plan that cannot fail! Satan tells Lana, "I want you to pick out two men, one in the political field and the other in religion. Set them up as world leaders then, when the time is right, I will enter one of them just like I did Judas Iscariot. Then I WILL RULE THE WORLD!" Even as unseen entities take over the world, the majority of people are unaware of what is going on.

If these books are not yet available in your local bookstore, order them direct by e-mail, calling, or faxing our Tampa office.

Warfare Plus Ministries offers many tape series on special demonic warfare issues and mini-books on individual stronghold forces. For a listing of our ministry tapes, manuals and other materials, visit our web site or write to us. You may also request a product order form at the same address.

If you are interested in attending a group seminar or want to schedule a group seminar in your local church, please call or write to us. Be sure to also request *The Battle Report,* the free newsletter from Warfare Plus Ministries.

Paul and Claire Hollis
Warfare Plus Ministries, Inc.
PMB #206 • 4577 Gunn Highway
Tampa, FL 33624 USA
(813) 265-2379 • Fax : (813) 908-0228
E-mail: WarfareP@aol.com
Web Site: www.warfareplus.com

Product Number	Description	Quantity	Unit Price	Total Cost
	BOOKS			
WP-101	This Means War		$12.95	
WP-102	Demon Slayers		$11.95	
WP-103	The Light		$11.95	
WP-104	Delayed Invasion		$11.95	
WP-105	Deceived		$12.95	
	AUDIOS			
WP-201	Expose & Expel Demon Power (4 Tapes)		$20.00	
WP-202	Inner Healing/Spiritual D. (4 Tapes)		$20.00	
WP-203	Don't Get Caught In Satan's Web		$10.00	
WP-204	Are You Cursed? (2 Tapes)		$10.00	
WP-205	Power & Authority Over Evil (2 Tapes)		$10.00	
WP-206	If I'm Supposed To Be Gay ...(2 Tapes)		$10.00	
	VIDEOS			
WP-301	Expose & Expel (4 Videos)		$80.00	
WP-302	Inner Healing/Spiritual D. (4 Videos)		$80.00	
WP-303	Deliverance From Satan's Torment		$20.00	
	WORKBOOKS			
WP-401	Expose & Expel Demon Power		$20.00	
WP-402	Inner Healing/Spiritual Deliverance		$20.00	
WP-403	New Beginnings In Jesus Christ		$20.00	
			SUB TOTAL	
			Shipping & handling (see chart)	
			TOTAL	

Method Of Payment:
- ☐ Visa
- ☐ MasterCard
- ☐ Check

Credit Card Number: ______________

Expiration Date: ________

Shipping & Handling	
$10.00 & Less	$3.00
$10.01-25.00	$4.00
$25.02-40.00	$5.00
$40.01-60.00	$6.00
$60.01-75.00	$7.00
$75.01 or more	$9.00
USA RATES	

Please Print Clearly

Name ______________________
Address ______________________
City ______________________
State ________
Zip __________

Send To:
Warfare Plus Ministries
4577 Gunn Highway, PMB 206
Tampa, FL 33624

Fax: (813) 908-0228
E-Mail: WarfareP@aol.com